His name is Evan Michael Tanner. He is thirty-four years old and he hasn't slept a wink since a piece of shrapnel destroyed the sleep center in his brain during the Korean War.

Tanner loves lost causes and beautiful women. The FBI has a thick file on him; the CIA taps his phone. And a super-secret intelligence agency wants him to be their man.

But this time Tanner is working only for himself, stirred by the memory of an eighteen-year-old virgin who once shared his bed but spurned his offers of love. Now the time has come to rescue her — and face the reality that she is a virgin no more...

"Block generates nonstop suspense."

— PUBLISHERS WEEKLY

LAWRENCE BLOCK

HERE COMES A HERO

A JOVE BOOK

This Jove book contains the complete
text of the original edition.

HERE COMES A HERO

A Jove Book / published by arrangement with
the author

PRINTING HISTORY
Fawcett Publications edition published 1968
Jove edition / December 1985

ISBN: 0-515-08420-4

Jove books are published by The Berkley Publishing Group,
200 Madison Avenue, New York, N.Y. 10016.
The words "A JOVE BOOK" and the "J" with sunburst
are trademarks belonging to Jove Publications, Inc.

PRINTED IN THE UNITED STATES OF AMERICA

HERE COMES A HERO

Chapter One

❀ ❀ ❀

*At 2:30 one fine October afternoon I ripped the tele-*phone out of the wall. Minna said, "Evan, you have ripped the telephone out of the wall."

I looked at her. Minna is seven years old and looks like a Lithuanian edition of *Alice in Wonderland,* all blond and big-eyed, and it is generally a pleasure to look at her. Now, though, something in my glance told her that coexistence was temporarily impossible.

"I think I shall go to the park," she said carefully. "With Mikey."

"Mikey is in school."

"He stayed home today, Evan. It is a Jewish holiday."

Mikey, né Miguel, belonged to no church in particular and was thus free to become an ex-officio member of whatever religious group was staying home from school on any given day. I said something caustic about Mikey and the many paths to divine enlightenment. Minna asked if we had any stale bread, and I told her I couldn't be expected to keep track of that sort of thing, that kitchen inventories were her problem. She reappeared with three slices of bread for the pigeons. They didn't look especially stale.

"Good afternoon," she said in Lithuanian. "I forgive you for the intemperance of your mood, and trust you will be better suited to discourse upon my return."

She ducked out the door before I could chuck a shoe at her. Minna always speaks Lithuanian when she does her queen shtik. She has the right, after all. As the sole surviving descendant of Mindaugas, the first and only king of independent Lithuania, she is unquestionably a royal person. She has vowed to make me her prime minister upon the restoration of the Lithuanian monarchy, and I keep her promise in a drawer with my Czarist bonds and Confederate money.

So I sighed heavily, and Minna went off to poison the pigeons in the park, and I sighed again and got a screwdriver and opened up the little telephone thing on the wall and put the phone together again. There's much to be said for venting one's anger upon inanimate objects, especially when they are so readily repaired.

It took perhaps ten minutes to rewire the telephone, just a fraction of the time the little black monster had already cost me that day. It had been ringing intermittently since five in the morning. Since I do not sleep, friends and enemies feel free to call me at all hours, and this was one of those days when they had been doing precisely that.

I was devoting the day to working on a thesis on color symbolism in the nature poems of William Wordsworth, and if you think that sounds slightly dull you don't know the half of it. It was not at all the sort of thesis topic I would have selected, but for unknowable reasons it was precisely the sort of thesis topic Karen Dietrich had selected. Miss Dietrich was a schoolteacher in Suffolk County who would receive a raise in pay if she earned a master's degree. I in turn would receive $1000 for furnishing Miss Dietrich with an acceptable thesis, said thesis to run approximately twenty thousand words, making my words worth a nickel apiece, color symbolism notwithstanding.

Anyway, I had to finish the damned thing, and the phone kept ringing. For a while I gave Minna the job of answering it, a task she does rather well most of the time. This wasn't one of those times. Minna is fluent in

Lithuanian, Lettish, English, Spanish, and French, can struggle through in German and Armenian, picked up shreds of Irish last summer in Dublin, and knows occasional obscenities in perhaps half a dozen other tongues. So all morning long the phone kept ringing and Minna kept answering it and various clowns kept coming at her in Polish and Serbo-Croat and Italian and other languages outside her ken.

Until ultimately I ripped the damn thing out of the wall and Minna fled to cooler climes. And when the clime in my apartment cooled somewhat, I repaired the telephone. As you now know.

It was one of the major mistakes of my life.

For almost an hour the phone remained stoically silent. I probed Wordsworth and pounded my typewriter while the silent phone lulled me into a false sense of security. Then it rang and I answered it and a voice I did not recognize said, "Mr. Tanner? Mr. Evan Tanner?"

I said, "Yes."

"You don't know me, Mr. Tanner."

"Oh."

"But I have to talk to you."

"Oh."

"My name is Miriam Horowitz."

"How do you do, Miss Horowitz."

"It's Mrs. Horowitz. Mrs. Benjamin Horowitz."

"How do you do, Mrs. Horowitz."

"He's dead."

"Pardon me?"

"Benjamin, he should rest in peace. I am a widow."

"I'm very worry."

"Oh, it'll be eight years in February. What am I saying? Nine years. Nine years in February. Never sick a day, a hard worker, a good husband, he comes home tired from the office, like a candle he drops dead. It was his heart."

I changed ears so that Mrs. Horowitz could talk into the other one. She had fallen silent. I decided she needed prompting. "I'm Evan Tanner," I said.

"I know."

"You called me, Mrs. Horowitz. I don't want to, uh, be brusque with you, uh, but——"

"I'm calling you about my daughter."

I'm calling you about my daughter. There are bachelors in their middle thirties who can hear those words without erupting in panic, but they generally wear pink silk shorts and subscribe to physical culture magazines. I felt a well nigh irresistible urge to hang up the phone.

"My daughter Deborah. She's in trouble."

My daughter Deborah. She's in trouble.

I hung up the phone.

Deborah Horowitz is pregnant, I thought. Deborah Horowitz is pregnant, and her idiot of a mother has decided that Evan Michael Tanner is personally responsible for this state of affairs, and is presently measuring him for a son-in-law suit. Or a paternity suit.

I stood up and began pacing the floor. Now how in God's name, I wondered, had Deborah Horowitz managed to get pregnant? Why didn't she take her pills? What was the matter with her? And—

Wait a minute.

I didn't *know* anyone named Deborah Horowitz.

The phone rang. I picked it up, and Mrs. Horowitz's voice was saying something about our having been disconnected. I broke in to tell her that there was some sort of mistake, that I didn't even know her daughter.

"You're Evan Tanner?"

"Yes, but—"

"West 107th Street? Manhattan?"

"Yes, but—"

"You know her. And you have to help me, I'm a widow, I'm all alone in the world, I have nowhere to turn. You—"

"But—"

"You know her. Maybe you don't know her by her real name. Young girls, they always get fancy ideas about names. I remember when I was sixteen all of a sudden Miriam was no good, I had to call myself Mimi. Hah!"

"Your daughter—"

"Phaedra, she calls herself now."

I said slowly, softly, "Phaedra Harrow."

"See? You know her."

"Phaedra Harrow."

"The ideas they get. Both names, from Deborah to Phaedra and from Horowitz to —"

"Mrs. Horowitz," I said.

"Yes."

"Mrs. Horowitz, I think you've made a mistake." I took a deep breath. "If Phaedra—if Deborah, that is, if she's, uh, pregnant, well, I think it's impossible."

"What are you talking about?"

"I mean, if that's the case, I think you'd better start looking for a very bright star in the East. Because—"

"Who said anything about pregnant?"

"You did."

"In trouble, I said."

"Oh." I thought for a moment. "So you did."

"Her name wasn't good enough for her, she had to change it. Her country wasn't good enough for her, she had to go overseas. God knows what she gets mixed up in. I always get letters, and then the letters stop, and then I get this one postcard. Mr. Tanner, I'll tell you frankly, I'm frightened for her life. Mr. Tanner, let me tell you—"

I didn't hang up. I said, "Mrs. Horowitz, maybe we shouldn't go into this on the phone."

"No?"

"My phone is tapped."

"Oh, God!"

I thought her reaction might be a little extreme. When one is a recognized subversive, the unashamed member of any number of organizations pledged to the violent overthrow of one government or another, one learns to regard every telephone as tapped until proven otherwise. The Central Intelligence Agency maintains a permanent tap on my telephone, and the Federal Bureau of Investigation reads my mail. Or perhaps it's the other way around. I can never remember.

"I have to see you," Mrs. Horowitz said.

"Well, I'm sort of busy—"

"This is a matter of life or death."

"Well, I have this thesis I'm writing, you see, on, uh—"

"You know where I live, Tanner?"

"No."

"In Mamaroneck. You know Mamaroneck?"

"Well—"

She gave me the address. I didn't bother writing it down. "You'll come right up to me," she said. "I have everything here. I am waiting with my heart in my head."

She hung up, and a few minutes later so did I.

"I have never been on a train before," Minna said. She was squinting through a very dirty window, watching the very dirty East Bronx roll by. "Thank you for bringing me, Evan. This is a beautiful train."

Actually it was a terrible train. It was a commuter local of the New York, New Haven and Hartford, and it had left Grand Central a few minutes after five, and some minutes after that Minna and I had boarded it at the 125th Street station. Soon, albeit not soon enough, it would deposit us in Mamaroneck.

I had not really planned to be on this train or any other. I didn't take down Mrs. Horowitz's address for that very reason. Mrs. Horowitz on the phone was less than a pleasure, and Mrs. Horowitz face to face promised to be even worse. If Phaedra was in trouble—and God knows she deserved to be—I was fully confident she could land on her feet. Mothers like Mrs. Horowitz with daughters like Phaedra are always worried, and they usually have every right to be, but when they try to do something about it they almost invariably make matters worse.

"I don't see any animals," Minna said.

"You won't. That's the Bronx."

"I thought we would see the Bronx Zoo."

Minna has an insatiable passion for zoos. I gave her a brief geography lesson on the Bronx. I don't think she paid much attention, because she went on to tell me how she had gone to the Bronx Zoo with Kitty Bazerian once, and how Arlette Sazerac took her to the zoo in Dublin when we were over there, and how she had several times permitted Phaedra to accompany her to the children's zoo in Central Park. Minna has an uncanny knack for conning people into undertaking such excursions. I often suspect that she thinks I fall in love solely to provide her with zoo-takers.

I closed my eyes and thought about William Wordsworth, which was something I had been unable to do since the conversation with Phaedra's mother. Instead, I had passed the better part of two hours staring at the sheet of paper in my typewriter and thinking about Phaedra. I kept telling myself that there was nothing to worry about, and certainly nothing that I could do anyway. But the fact remained that one of the things I too obviously couldn't do was concentrate on the damned thesis while my mind was busy brooding over the possible whereabouts of an eighteen-year-old virgin with an incredible body, an implausible name, and an impenetrable chastity.

Phaedra Harrow. She came into my life, or I into hers, at a party held by the Ad Hoc Garbage for Greece Committee. Back in February the New York landscape had consisted of garbage, tons upon tons of garbage, its collection waiting upon the settlement of the sanitation workers' strike. Somebody is always on strike in New York, and this time it was the garbage men. The city was hip-deep in potato peelings and empty plastic containers, and packs of rats left sinking tenements to forage in the streets. It is perhaps illustrative of the current state of New York that the strike was three days old before anyone noticed the difference.

In any case, a group of prominent Greek-Americans, including one actress and twelve restauranteurs, took it upon themselves to organize the Garbage for Greece operation. It was conceived as a sort of viable alternative to Care packages; for five dollars one could send ten pounds of garbage to Athens, thus helping clean up New York and expressing one's feelings toward the Greek military junta in one swell foop.

Well. In ten days the strike was settled, with the result that the program never got off the ground (although the garbage did, finally). I don't think much more would have happened anyway. The main idea had been to garner a little newspaper space—very little, sad to say. But the group had retained its *espirit de corps,* and the night before Easter the group was throwing a party to celebrate the end of winter. And the party itself was an unqualified success. The membership of the New York chapter of the Pan-Hellenic Friendship Society was present in full force. The founders of the committee bankrupted their respective restaurants to provide food and drink. There was lamb roasted in every possible fashion, pilafs of rice and pine nuts and currants, fluffy and gooey confections of dough and walnuts and honey. And there was wine.

Lord, was there wine! Case upon case of retsina and rhoditys and mavrodaphne, wine to sip along with the food, wine to swallow along with the fiery speeches, wine to swill while George Pappas plucked his oud and Stavros Melchos pounded his copper drum and Kitty Bazerian offered up a furious dance as tribute to the cause of Hellenic (and sexual) freedom.

Phaedra Harrow. She stood in a corner of the cavernous banquet room drinking retsina from a half-gallon jug. Her hair was a glossy dark-brown waterfall flowing down her back almost to her waist, which in turn was small, which the rest of her emphatically was not. She wore what was either the ultimate miniskirt or a rather wide cummerbund. Her legs began precisely where this garment left off; clad snugly in green mesh tights, they ran a well-shaped course to her feet, which were tucked into a pair of green suede toes-turned-up slippers of the sort cobblers make for elves. Her sweater had been designed to drape loosely, but it had not been designed with Phaedra in mind. It fit snugly.

I saw her from halfway across the room, and I stared at her until she looked my way, and our eyes locked as eyes are wont to do. I walked to her. She passed me the jug of wine, and I drank, and she drank, and we looked into each other's eyes. Hers were the color of her hair, almond-shaped, very large. Mine are nothing remarkable.

"I am Evan Tanner," I said. "And you are a creature of myth and magic."

"I am Phaedra."

"Phaedra," I said. "Sister to Ariadne, bride to Theseus. And hast thou killed the minotaur? Come to my arms, my beamish boy."

"O frabjous day," said Phaedra.

"And would you hang yourself for love of Hippolytus? He's naught but a loutish lad and hardly worthy of your attentions. Do you believe in love at first sight?"

"And second and third."

"Phaedra. Easter is upon us, and Phaedra has put an end to winter. Now is the winter of our discotheque—ah, you laugh, but that's the real meaning of Easter. The rebirth of the world, Christ is risen, and the sap rises in the trees. Do you know that just a dozen blocks from here Easter will be properly celebrated? There's a Russian Orthodox church where they do this particular holiday superbly. Singing and shouting and joy. Come, my Phaedra. This party is dying around us"—a lie, it went on exuberantly for another five hours—"and we've just time to catch the midnight Easter service, and I love you, you know—"

The Russian services were glorious. They were still in progress when we left the church around two. We found a diner on 14th Street and drank coffee with our mouths and each other with our eyes. I asked her where she was from, where she was living. She quoted Omar: "I came like water and like wind I go." And, more specifically, she said that she did not presently have any place to stay. She had been living with some hippies on East 10th Street but had moved out that afternoon; everyone was high all the time,

she said, and nobody really did anything, and she had had
enough of that sort of thing.

"Come to my place," I said.

"All right."

"Come live with me and be my love."

"Yes."

And as our taxi raced from the Lower East Side to the
Upper West Side, she settled her head on my shoulder. "I
have things to tell you," she said. "I am Phaedra Harrow.
I am eighteen years old."

"Half my age. Do you believe in numerology? I think
the implications are fascinating—"

"I am a virgin."

"That's extraordinary."

"I know."

"Uh—"

Her hand pressed my arm. "I am not anti-sex or frigid or
a lesbian or anything. And I don't want to be seduced or
talked into it. People try all the time—"

"That's not hard to believe."

"—but it's not what I want. Not now. I want to see the
whole world. I want to find things out, I want to grow.
I'm talking too much now. When I drink too much I talk
too much. But I want you to understand this. I would like
to stay with you, to live with you, if you still want me to.
But I don't want to make love."

At the time, what I wondered most about this little
speech was whether Phaedra herself believed it. I certainly
didn't. I didn't even believe she was a virgin, for that
matter. I had long felt that the species was either mytholog-
ical or extinct, and that a virgin was a seven-year-old girl
who could run faster than her brother.

So all the way home I was certain I knew how we
would celebrate the coming of spring. I would convert my
couch into a bed, and I would take this fine, sweet,
magnificent girl in my arms, and, well, write in your own
purple passage.

The best laid plans of mice and men sometimes aren't.

Phaedra certainly wasn't. At my apartment I was shocked to discover that she really meant just what she had said. She was a virgin, and she intended to remain a virgin for the foreseeable future, and while she would willingly sleep with me with the understanding that we would do no more than share bed space in a platonic fashion, she would not countenance any sort of sexual involvement.

So I made the couch into a bed, all right, and I put her to sleep in it, and then I went into the kitchen and made myself some coffee and read several books without being able to pay much attention to them. A mood, I told myself. Or a monthly plague, or something. It would pass.

But it never did. Phaedra stayed at my apartment for just about a month, and it was as acutely frustrating a month as I have ever spent in my life. She was in every other respect a perfect house guest: absorbing company when I wanted company, perfectly unobstrusive when I had something to do, an ideal companion for Minna, a reasonable cook and housekeeper. If the delight that was Phaedra had been purely sexual, I would have quickly sent her away. If, on the other hand, I had not found her so overpoweringly attractive, I could have quickly adjusted to the sort of brother-sister relationship she wanted to maintain. Unless one possesses the mentality of a rapist, after all, one regards desire as an essentially mutual thing. Lust cannot long be a one-way street.

At least I had always found this to be the case. Now, though, it wasn't. Every day I found myself wanting the cloistered little bitch more, and every day it became more evident that I was not going to have her. The obvious solution—that I find some other female with a more realistic outlook on life and love—worked better in theory than in practice. I was not, sad to say, a horny adolescent who purely and simply wanted to get his ashes hauled. There are any number of ways to ameliorate such a problem, but mine was something else again. When lechery is specific, substitutes don't work at all; they make about as much sense as eating a loaf of bread when you're dying of thirst.

This went on twenty-four hours a day for a month, and if you think it sounds maddening, then perhaps you're beginning to get the point. After the first night Phaedra had moved into Minna's room and shared Minna's bed, so at least I didn't have to watch her sleep; but even at night the presence of her filled the apartment and addled my brain.

Yet I couldn't even talk to Phaedra about it, not at much length. Any conversation on the subject served only to heighten my frustration and her guilt feelings without bringing matters any closer to their logical conclusion.

"It's so wrong," she would say. "I can't stay here any more, Evan. You've been wonderful to me and it's just not fair to you. I'll move out."

And then I would have to talk her into staying. I was afraid if she moved out I would lose her. Sooner or later, I thought, she would either give in or I would cease to want her. It did not happen quite that way, however. Instead, I was like a man with an injured foot, limping automatically through life without being constantly conscious of the pain.

Hell. I wanted her and didn't get her, and by the end of the month I had grown used to this state of affairs, and then one day she said that she had to go away, that she was leaving New York. She wasn't sure where she was going. I felt a dual sense of loss and liberation. She was half my age, I told myself, and desperately neurotic, and her neurosis seemed to be contagious, and much as I loved her I was bloody well rid of her. So she moved out, and for a while the apartment was lonely, and then it wasn't. There was, briefly, a girl named Sonya.

And now it was the middle of October, the one month of the year when New York is at its best. The air has a crispness to it, and the wind changes direction and blows most of the pollution away, and on good days the sky has a distinct bluish cast to it. Spring had been drizzly and summer impossible and it stood to reason that winter, when it came, would be as bad as it always is, but this particular

October was the sort they had in mind when they wrote "Autumn in New York," and I had been looking forward to it for months.

So before the week was out I was on the other side of the Atlantic.

Chapter Two

❀ ❀ ❀

On my fourth day in London it rained. It had been doing this more or less constantly since my arrival, sometimes with fog as an accompaniment, sometimes without. I got back to the Stokes' flat a few minutes after six, rerolled the umbrella that Nigel Stokes insisted I carry, and went into the kitchen. Julia was hovering at the stove, and I hovered beside her, as much for the stove's warmth as for hers.

"I'm just getting tea," she said. "Nigel's shaving, I think. It's desperate out, isn't it?"

"Yes."

"How did it go?"

"No luck at all."

She was pouring the tea when her brother joined us. He was in his early forties, some ten years older than Julia. His guards' moustache, which added several years to his appearance, was a recent addition; he'd grown it for his role in a farce that had opened a few weeks ago in the West End, and planned to shave it off as soon as the play closed. From the reviews it seemed that this would happen rather soon.

"Well," he said. "Any luck?"

"None, I'm afraid."

"And bloody awful weather for hunting wild geese,

isn't it?" He added sugar to his tea, buttered a slice of bread. "Where'd you go today? More of the same?"

I nodded. "Travel agencies, employment agencies. And I went to half the rooming houses in Russell Square, and I suppose I did have a bit of luck. I found the last place she stayed before quitting London. She had a room around the corner from the museum. The dates fit; she checked out on the sixteenth of August. But she left no forwarding address, and no one there had any idea where she might have gone."

"It seems hopeless," Julia said.

That seemed a concise summation of the state of affairs—it seemed quite hopeless, and I was beginning to wonder why I had let myself be panicked into making the trip in the first place. One reason, of course, was the emotional state of Mrs. Horowitz. Alarm is contagious, and the woman was profoundly alarmed. But it was also true that Phaedra's letters did nothing to dispel this alarm. There was the last letter from England: *I can't tell you much for security reasons, but I have this fantastic opportunity to travel through lands I never even hoped to see. I wish I could tell you more about it.* And a postcard of the Victoria and Albert Museum, mailed from Baghdad and with an indecipherable date with this chilling scrawl: *Everything's gone wrong. Am in real trouble. You may never hear from me again. Hope I can mail this.* Evidently she had been in so much trouble that she had neither pen nor pencil; the message was in charcoal.

I don't remember what I told Mrs. Horowitz. I calmed her as well as I could, then took Minna back to the apartment, disconnected the telephone, and worked non-stop on the thesis for three days and two nights. I speeded things up by fabricating most of the footnotes. Karen Dietrich paid me my thousand dollars. I cashed her check while the ink was still drying, put the bills in my money belt and the belt around my waist, threw things into a flight bag, boarded a reluctant Minna at Kitty Bazerian's in Brooklyn, considered and rejected risking a direct flight to London, and caught—with less than ten minutes to spare—an Aer Lingus jet to Shannon and Dublin.

The British government has my name on several lists, and I had a feeling they might give me a hard time. The Irish also have me listed as a subversive—I'm a member of the Irish Republican Brotherhood—but they don't make a fuss about that sort of thing. Since most people are trying to get out of the country, they've never been able to take illegal entry very seriously.

But all I saw of Ireland was the inside of Dublin Airport. I had breakfast there before catching a BEA flight to London. You don't have to show a passport to get from Ireland to England. The flight was routine, except for the casual regurgitation of several babes in arms, and in due course I was in London and on my way to Nigel Stokes' flat in Kings Cross.

And I was still there. I had corresponded with Nigel over the years and met him once in New York when a play of his made a brief appearance on Broadway. He was a fellow member of the Flat Earth Society and had been working for years to build an elaborate true-to-scale two-dimensional globe, a project I greatly admired. Julia didn't. She thought the whole thing was madness. Nigel damn well knew it was madness, and took great delight in it.

And now, pouring us each a second cup of tea, he said, "This is madness, you know." But he wasn't talking about the shape of the earth.

"I know."

"It's bad enough looking through haystacks for needles, but you don't really know that it's a needle you're hunting, do you? I was thinking about that letter, Evan. Somehow I don't think a travel agent—"

I nodded. "I've been keeping busy, that's all."

"Quite. And employment bureaus—oh, that's possible, of course, but somehow I don't think you'll have much luck. It's rather a case of going around Robin Hood's barn, isn't it?"

"It is," I agreed.

Julia drew up a chair and sat down between us. "Have you thought of going to Baghdad?"

"That's ridiculous," her brother said. "Where would he begin looking in Baghdad?"

I closed my eyes. He was right—it would be quite pointless to try looking for Phaedra in Baghdad. And Julia, for her part, seemed able to read minds, because I had been thinking of doing just that, ridiculous or no.

Nigel stroked his moustache. "Perhaps I've been seeing too many films, but— Evan, let me see that letter again, will you?" I quoted it to him by rote. "Yes, I thought so. You know, I get the impression of some sort of cloak-and-dagger operation here, don't you? Spies and such, midnight rides on the Orient Express. What do you think?"

"Mmmm," I said neutrally. The same thought had occurred to me, but I had tried to suppress it. Some time ago I found myself working for a nameless man who heads a nameless U.S. undercover operation. I'm not being coy—I don't know his name or its. Since then he's been under the impression that I work for him, and now and then I do. For that reason, thoughts of cloaks and daggers come to mind rather more often than they ought to, and in this case I had discounted them.

But—

"Evan?" I looked up. "Now here you have a girl who'd come to London, where as far as we know she didn't know a soul. She might make friends, but—"

"But they wouldn't make her," I said.

"Pardon?"

"Nothing. Go on."

"Quite. Now I can't see MI 5 knocking on her door in Russell Square, can you? Nor do I think she'd have gone the rounds of the employment agencies, and I don't suppose she had much money—"

"Probably not."

"—so I wonder if she mightn't have answered a Personal in the *Times*. Had you thought of that?"

"No." I straightened up. "I should have thought of that myself. We would want the issues for the first two weeks

in August. I suppose the newspaper offices have them on
file, or is there a library that—"

"Courtney," Julia said.

"Why, of course," Nigel said. "Courtney Bede." He
turned to me. "There's an old fellow who keeps every
issue of the *Times*. And all the other papers as well. He's
what you would call a character. Quite daft, actually, but
not a bad sort. Do you want to go round there?"

The English have certain words that are better than
ours. *Daft* is one of them. Such American alternatives as
flaky don't quite do the job.

Courtney Bede was daft. He was a short, round man
who might have been anywhere from fifty to ninety—it
was quite impossible to tell. He performed some backstage
function in the theater and lived alone in a basement
apartment in Lambeth not far from the Old Vic. There, in
four sizable rooms, he existed as a rather orderly version
of the Collier brothers.

He saved things. He saved string, and empty bottles,
and bits of metal, and theater programs, and keys that
didn't fit anything, and all of the items that most people
throw out. His collections, which he showed me with more
pride than I thought justified, did not really thrill me as
much as he felt they should. But he did have newspapers,
all right. Ten years' worth of all of the London papers,
stacked neatly in piles by date.

"And not one of 'em cost me a ha'penny," he said,
poking out his stomach for emphasis. "London's full of
fools and spendthrifts, lad. Men and women what'll pay
sixpence for a paper and throw it away after a single
reading. I get all me papers every day, and not one of 'em
that costs me a ha'penny."

"And you read all the papers yourself?"

"Oh, I'll give a glance at one now and then. Mondays
I'll generally have a look at Sunday's *News of the World*.
But it's not the reading of 'em, it's the having that does for
me."

I told him the issues we wanted. This August was easy,

he said, but if it was two or three Augusts ago we wanted it wouldn't take ten minutes to dig 'em out for us. He found the issues, and Nigel and I divided them up and went through the long columns of personal ads. There were endless appeals for donations to obscure charities, odd coded notices, occasional sex solicitations by self-styled models, palmists, strict governesses, *et al.* And, ultimately there was this:

> YOUNG WOMEN—an opportunity for adventure and foreign travel with generous remuneration. Applicants must be unattached, security minded. Apply in person, Carradine, No. 67, Great Portland Street. Discretion expected and assured.

"It needn't be that," Nigel pointed out. "Might be any of these we checked, you know. 'Companion wanted for journey to Continent,' anything of that sort."

"Still ..."

"Yes, it does look promising. Damn, I've got to get to the theater. If you'd like, I'll go round to Great Portland Street with you in the morning."

"I'll go now."

"I shouldn't think they'd be open, actually."

"I don't even think they exist," I said. "That's what I want to find out."

The building on Great Portland Street housed a dealer in coins and medals on the ground floor, with the other four floors broken up into a variety of small offices, all of which were closed for the day. The name Carradine did not appear either on the directory posted on the first floor or on any of the office doors. I waited in the coin and medal shop while a small boy and his father selected several shillings' worth of small foreign coins. The transaction took an inordinate amount of time, and when it was finally completed the clerk seemed relieved that I didn't want to buy anything. "Carradine," he said. "Carradine,

Carradine. Would that be a Mr. Carradine, do you suppose, or the name of the establishment?" I told him his guess was as good as mine, if not better. "Carradine," he said again. "August, you say. First fortnight of August. Would you excuse me for a moment, sir? I'll ask our Mr. Talbot."

He disappeared into the back, then reappeared a few moments later. "If you'll step into the back room, sir, our Mr. Talbot will see you."

Our Mr. Talbot was a red-faced man with uncommonly large ears. He sat at a rolltop desk dipping coins into a glass of clear liquid and wiping them on a soft rag. The solution, whatever it was, managed to turn the coins bright and silvery while staining the tips of our Mr. Talbot's fingers dark brown.

"Carradine," he said. "Never met the gentleman, but I do recall the name. Late summer, I think. Don't believe he was here long. Have you tried the owner?"

I hadn't. He gave me a name and address and telephone number, and I thanked him. He said, "Not a collector, are you?" I admitted that I wasn't. He grunted and resumed dipping coins. I thanked the clerk on the way out and called the building's owner from a booth down the block.

A voice assured me the man was out and no one knew when he might be returning. I thought for a moment, then called again and announced that I was an inquiry agent interested in the whereabouts of a former tenant. The same voice introduced itself as the owner. Evidently he'd been avoiding some tenant who wanted his office painted; landlords, after all, are the same the whole world over.

He told me what I wanted to know. A Mr. T. R. Smythe-Carson had taken a third-floor office under the name of Carradine Imports in late July, paid a month's rent in advance, left before the month was over, and provided no forwarding address.

For form's sake, I looked for Smythe-Carson in the telephone directory. He wasn't there, and I wasn't surprised.

There are some nights when I envy those who sleep. I have not slept since World War 2.1, when a sliver of North Korean shrapnel entered my mind and found its way to something called the sleep center, whereupon I entered a state of permanent insomnia. I was eighteen when this happened, and by now I can barely remember what sleep was like.

In the past few years scientists have taken an interest in sleep. They've been trying to determine just why people sleep, and what dreams do, and what happens when a person is prevented from sleeping and dreaming. I could probably answer a few of their questions. When a person is prevented from sleeping and dreaming he embraces a wide variety of lost causes, studies dozens of languages, eats five or six meals a day, and uses his life to furnish those elements of fantasy that other men find in dreams. This may not be how it works for every absolute insomniac, but it's how it works for the only absolute insomniac I know, and for the most part I'm quite happy with it. After all, why waste eight hours a night sleeping when, with proper application, one can waste all twenty-four wide awake?

Yet there are times when sleep would be a pleasure, if only because it provides a subjectively speedy way to get from one day to the next when there is absolutely nothing else to do. This was one of those times. Nigel and Julia had repaired to their separate bedrooms. There was no one in London whom I wanted to see. The hunt for Smythe-Carson and Carradine would have to wait until morning. Meanwhile . . .

Meanwhile what?

Meanwhile I bathed and shaved and put on reasonably clean clothes and drank tea with milk and sugar and fried up some eggs and bacon and read part of a collection of the *Best Plays of 1954* (which were none too good) and stretched out on my back on the floor for twenty minutes of Yoga-style relaxation. This last involves flexing and relaxing muscle groups in turn, then blanking the mind through a variety of mental disciplines. The mind-blanking part of it was easier than usual this time because my mind was very nearly empty to begin with.

Then I read fifty pages of an early Eric Ambler novel, at which point I remembered how it ended. Then I picked up that morning's copy of the London *Times,* which I had already read once, which is generally enough. I had a go at the bridge and chess columns and the garden news, and then I turned to the Personals. Halfway down the first column it occurred to me that I had a particular reason to check out the Personals, and halfway down the third column I found the reason.

> IF YOU ARE female, under 40, unmar-
> ried, intelligent, adventurous, free to travel,
> opportunity awaits you! Do not mention
> this ad to others but reply in person at
> Penzance Export, No. 31, Pelham Court,
> Marylebone.

"Of course it's Smythe-Carson again," Nigel said the next morning. "Quite the same sort of message, isn't it? He's stopped mentioning the high pay and has——"

"And has abandoned Carradine in favor of Penzance," Julia put in.

"And Smythe-Carson for something else, no doubt. And took new offices, but hasn't left Marylebone. I don't know just where Pelham Court is, Evan. Julia?"

I said, "I was there last night."

"No one home, I don't suppose?"

"No. The building was locked." I had guessed it would be, but I found the ad around 3:30 and had four hours to kill before Nigel and Julia would get up, and there are times when pointless activity is preferable to inactivity.

"So whatever he was doing before——"

"He's doing it again," I said.

"I wonder what it is."

I stood up. "Whatever it is, I'll find out soon enough. And I'll find out just what the hell happened to Phaedra, and——"

"How?"

I looked down at Julia. "Why, I'll ask him, I suppose."

"But don't you suppose he's bent?" I looked puzzled. "I'm sorry, you people say crooked, don't you?"

"Oh." Two countries, I thought, divided by a single language. "I'm certain he's working some sort of racket. Oh." I nodded slowly. "For the past few days I had operated on the vague assumption that Phaedra had gone on a tour or taken some form of legitimate employment, after which something went awry. Thus I had shown her photograph to travel agents and employment agencies and had inquired after her by both of her names, in the full expectation of getting an honest answer to an honest question. That line wouldn't work with Mr. Smythe-Carson.

"You might call the police," Nigel suggested.

I thought it over. But if S-C was working a racket, or playing some version of foreign intrigue, it was more than possible that Phaedra was involved to a point where official attention might be a bad idea. Besides, I wasn't entirely certain how I stood with the police—they might turn out to be displeased with my presence in their country.

"I could go round if you'd like," Nigel went on. "Pass myself off as an inspector from the Yard. I've played the bloody part often enough, and the moustache would go well with the role. Or do you think that would just put the wind up him?"

"It might."

"Or I could disguise myself as female, under forty, unmarried. Somehow I don't think that would wash. You might do some sort of exploratory research, Evan. Inquiring about the position on behalf of a female relative, that sort of thing. Give you the feel of the man—"

Julia said, "Of course you've both overlooked the obvious."

We looked at her.

"You ought to send an unmarried female under forty to find out exactly what's going on. Fortunately I know just the girl. She's had a bit of acting experience, she's considered moderately attractive and intelligent, and she's bloody adventurous." She stood up, a thin smile on her freshly scrubbed face, a light dancing in her eyes. "I hereby volunteer my services," she said.

So of course we both told her that it was a ridiculous idea, not to say dangerous, not to mention foolhardy. We pointed out that she might compromise herself in any of a number of ways and added that we could not possibly let her risk herself in such a fashion.

And, of course, three hours later I was looking through a tea shop window on Pelham Court, waiting for her to return from the offices of Penzance Export just across the street.

"It does restore a girl's confidence," she said. We were having lunch at a Lyon's Corner House a few blocks away from Penzance Export. "One regards oneself as utterly dependent upon the stray pence one ekes out playing chambermaids in bedroom farces, along with the meager income from a legacy and the generosity of one's brother. At nights I often comfort myself with the thought that I could always turn brass if times went bad, but who would have me?"

"I would."

"Oh?" She arched her eyebrows prettily. "You'll be my first professional client, I promise you." Her voice turned at once Cockney and sluttish. "Spare a couple of nicker for a short time, guv?" She laughed. "But I digress, don't I? Mr. Wyndham-Jones has hired me. He seems partial to hyphenated surnames. A low type, I'm afraid. Speaks straight Mayfair, but Whitechapel shines through in spite of all his hard work."

"And he hired you."

"He certainly did." She grinned suddenly. "I wish you could have been there, Evan. I wish Nigel could have been there. Whenever I'm on stage and he's in the house I'm just dreadful, and this was the performance of my

career. I did a Yorkshire accent"—she demonstrated this
—" and I told him my old father had just died and I was
quite alone in the world and new in London and I did so
want to travel. I made myself the wide-eyed trusting sort,
just a shade on the stupid side, but I tried to give the
impression that I kept my own counsel and wouldn't be
inclined to confide in anyone." She sighed. "It worked. I
shall be leaving the country at the end of the week for a
three-month journey through the Middle East. All of my
expenses will be paid and I will receive three hundred
pounds at the termination of the trip."

"The Middle East. Phaedra's card was from Baghdad."

"Yes. The mission's a lovely one. Shall I tell you about
it? Mr. Wyndham Hyphen Jones will be posing as the
leader of an archaeological expedition to Turkey and Iraq.
An archaeological tour, really. But in actual point of fact,
the six or seven girls accompanying him on this trek will
not be his passengers but his employees. Or, more precisely, the employees of a we-cannot-mention-the-name mam-
moth oil company with interests in the area. It will be our
vital task to Gather Important Information and Make
Necessary Contacts. Isn't that divine?"

"More divine than plausible."

"Quite. I don't suppose you've any idea what his real
game is? He knows I've no money at all. I read thrillers,
so all manner of horrid things have occurred to me, but
nothing makes any sense."

"Six or seven pretty but penniless girls. Maybe he's a
sex fiend."

"Just a fiend, I think. I can generally tell when a man
responds to me that way. For example, you do, don't
you?"

"Uh . . ."

"Why, you've gone tongue-tied! If it's a comfort, I react
the same way to you. But Mr. Hyphen—I watched him
study me and decide I was attractive without taking the
slightest personal interest in the fact. He might enjoy
slitting my throat, but I'm afraid that's the only way I
could give him any pleasure." She shivered, then grinned

quickly. "Theatrical response indicating chills and palpitations. Mr. Hyphen strikes me as evil incarnate. Wait until you see him."

"I can't wait."

"Will tonight do? I've a date to meet him at his flat."

"What!"

"Color me resourceful. I'd already told him I was penniless, so I thought I'd press it a bit. I hit him up for a tenner on account. He allowed that he'd left his billfold in his other pair of trousers. Quite a transparent fellow—I don't believe he has another pair of trousers, let alone a spare ten quid. I'm to meet him at his flat at half past eight this evening. He'll have my ten pounds, along with an employment application for me to fill out."

"You have the address?"

"Old Compton Street in Soho."

"You're not going, of course."

She rose. "Let's go back to the flat, Evan. I'm going to Old Compton Street tonight, but my damned brother's going to voice the same objections as you, and I'd as soon save time by arguing with both of you at once."

The argument wasn't much of a contest. She had logic on her side, and when Nigel turned out to be easily won over I couldn't put up much of a fight. I'd planned on keeping the appointment for her, but there was really no reason to presume he would let me in. There was also the chance that he would have company, which would make the odds unfavorable for our side.

With Julia running interference for me, we hedged our bets neatly. She could signal to let me know that she was alone, and I could wait in the hallway, prepared to enter when he let her out. Nor would she be in any real danger; whatever his intentions, I'd be lying doggo in the hallway ready to kick the door in if she screamed.

Julia said, "But suppose he won't talk?"

We looked at her.

"He might not, you know. It would be rather like going

to his office and waving pictures under his nose, wouldn't it?"

"Evan will have a gun, dear." He turned to me. "I can pick you up one from the property department. It won't shoot, but I don't suppose you want to shoot anyone. I'll guarantee that it looks menacing."

"But if he refuses to talk, then what?"

"Then Evan will make him talk, love."

"Oh, come now. That's a line out of the movies. I could believe that of Mr. Hyphen, but Evan's not a brutal sort." She put her hand on my arm. "Are you?"

I remembered a man named Kotacek, a Slovak Nazi, a doddering invalid who had not wanted to tell me where he kept his lists of the worldwide membership of the Neo-Nazi movement. It took a while, but he told me. I never behaved more inhumanly before or since, but then I'd never been faced with a more inhuman man.

"Brutal?" I said. "Everybody's brutal."

"Oh, Evan, for God's sake! Everybody's brutal and each man kills the thing he loves and life is real and life is earnest. But you know what I mean."

Nigel touched her shoulder. His guards' moustache fairly bristled. "You go too much by manner, love," he said quietly. "Brutal to him who brutal thinks. I've a feeling your Mr. Hyphen will tell Evan anything he wants to know."

Chapter Three

❀ ❀ ❀

Old Compton Street is no place to stand around waiting for something. It's in that part of Soho that's a cross between Greenwich Village and Tijuana—narrow streets jammed with Italian restaurants and strip clubs and pornography shops and prostitutes. I stood in front of a grim pub just across the street from the building where our hyphenated friend lived. I'd already determined that his apartment was in the front of the building on either the third or fourth floor, depending upon whether you looked at it from an English or American point of view. You had to climb three flights of stairs to get to it, anyway.

An urgent little man in a houndstooth jacket buttonholed me and at once provided me with a good reason for standing on the sidewalk. I stood waiting for Julia's taxi while he ran through his catalog of vice. "Looking for a girl, are you now, mate? Soho's full of girls, but you got to find the right sort, you know. Nice clean girl, young, white, just started in the business not two months ago. It's no good if you get one what ain't clean, but this is a choice bit of brass, very young and pretty——"

I put my hands in my pockets. I had a gun in each pocket and neither one could do much damage. The smaller one fired blanks, while the other, somewhat more realistic in appearance, was a single piece of cast iron.

35

Nigel had offered me my choice and I'd taken both of them.

"Care to see a blue film, mate? Just five nicker for a full show. A Yank, aren't you? That's twelve of your dollars. Used to be fourteen, but you get a break with the devaluation. Bargain day, isn't it? There's a full hour of films, new ones, some in color. A man and a woman, two men and a woman, a man and two women, two women together, a woman and a dog, a woman and—"

A taxi drew to a stop in front of the building I was watching. Julia got out of it and passed some coins to the driver. She went into the building and the cab stayed where it was. If Hyphen was by himself she would signal the driver, tipping me in the process.

"Sell you any bloody thing you want. French postcards, French ticklers, Spanish fly. Drugs I don't handle, but I know them what does. See a live show? Not strippers, but me and a girl, fucking and sucking and all, and then you can have her yourself or not, your choice, and all it costs—"

A shade went up in the Hyphen apartment. I saw Julia wave to her driver, who, as it happened, had already driven off with another fare. Then she lowered the shade again.

"And hoping you won't take offense, mate, but to each his own as they say, and would you fancy a young boy? You don't look the sort, but I always ask, and—"

I tucked my chin into my coat collar, pitched my voice low, and changed my American accent for an English one. "Special Branch," I murmured. "We don't bother with touts and ponces as a rule, but unless you bugger off quick I might make an exception in your case."

I kept my eyes on the ground as I said this, and when I looked up he was gone. I walked to the far corner, crossed the street, walked back to the doorway Julia had entered a few minutes earlier. No one seemed to be paying any particular attention to me. I went inside. The foyer wall displayed half a dozen three-by-five file cards—Model,

French Model, Spanish Model, with names and apartment numbers. I wondered what real models called themselves.

The apartments on the first two floors housed models exclusively. There were two apartments on the third floor, our friend's and one belonging to a model named Suzette. I suppose she had as much right to the name Suzette as he did to Wyndham-Jones. I put an ear to his door. I could hear voices, his and hers, but couldn't make out what they were saying. I stepped back, and the door of Suzette's apartment opened behind me and a man emerged. Suzette was close behind him, urging him to return soon. I turned to look at him, and he couldn't have been more anxious to avoid me if I had been his father-in-law the vicar. He plunged madly down the stairs. I turned to look at Suzette. Her bright red lips curled in a smile and she dropped one eyelid in a wink.

"Hope you weren't waiting long, love," she said. "The time he took, I ought to charge him by the hour." She had a little trouble with *h*'s. "Now don't be a shy one. Come inside and we'll get acquainted."

She was wearing a shiny wrapper the color of her lipstick, and she had so much pancake on her face that it was impossible to guess what she might look like without it. She couldn't have looked much worse.

"I'm waiting for a friend," I said.

"Are you now?" Again the wink. "Come inside and we'll wait together." She minced across the hallway at me. "Suzie'll show you a good time, ducks. You've no call to be bashful."

I had the awful feeling that as soon as she got close enough she would make a grab at my fly. I reached into my inside pocket and came up with my U.S. passport, flipped it open, and flashed it at her.

"Cor," she said. One hand flew to her throat. "I'm just a bleeding model, it's a respectable occupation—"

"Fifth Squad," I said. I have no idea what that is, or if there is one. "I'm backing up my partner, he's upstairs. Might be wise of you to stay inside."

Her eyes widened. "What's on?"

"Spies."

"Russians?"

I shrugged.

"Bleeding Communists," she said. She opened her door, ducked inside, then out again. "When you've done," she said, "you might stop in for a cuppa." Then she mercifully drew her door shut, and I put my passport away.

I stood there for another five minutes. At one point a midget passed me on his way downstairs. I tried not to guess where he had been or what he had been doing. Then I heard steps approaching Mr. Hyphen's door. I put both hands in my pockets, drew out both guns, and decided on the one with the blanks. I stood close to the wall alongside the door.

There was the sound of the bolt being drawn. Then the knob turned, and he opened the door and held it for Julia. I walked in as she came out, digging the nose of the pistol into his middle.

"All right," I said. "Back up now. Close the door, Julia. Now back off, friend, and turn around nice and slow, and keep your hands in the air."

He backed off, and he put his hands in the air, but he didn't turn around. He was my height, eight or ten years younger, and many pounds heavier. I saw at once what Julia meant about his eyes. They were cold, opaque, utterly lacking in depth. In my part of New York boys with eyes like that are very good with knives.

Slowly, his hands came down again. "Not bloody likely," he said. "You aren't about to shoot, are you, china?" Rhyming slang, I thought stupidly; china, china plate, mate. "Not a peeler, and there's not a pin here for stealing, so just who in bleeding hell are you?" He took a step toward me. "Better let me take that toy before you hurt yourself."

So I pointed the gun at his gut and fired.

It didn't sound much like a truck backfiring. What it sounded like was a .38-caliber automatic. For an instant it must have felt like that, too, because he fell back as if shot and stared down in horror at the spot in his middle where the bullet would have gone had the gun contained one.

His face had just begun to register the fact that he hadn't been shot when I took the other fake pistol, the cast-iron one, and bounced it off the side of his head.

I turned to Julia. She stood motionless and open-mouthed, a bronze casting entitled "Astonishment." "Get into the hall," I said. "You want to know where the shot came from; it sounded as though it came from upstairs. Remember what a fine actress you are. Hurry!"

She did a good job. I locked the door behind her and listened to the hubbub outside while I got Mr. Hyphen properly trussed up. There was a substantial stuffed chair with molded wooden arms. I wrestled him into it and used a roll of picture-hanging wire to fasten him in place, his arms to the chair's arms, his feet to its legs, and the rest of him to the back and seat of it. I was in a hurry, and that sort of work isn't my favorite diversion anyway—I can't wrap a Christmas present properly, let alone a person. So I don't suppose I did the sort of job that would have left Houdini hamstrung, but that wasn't the idea. I just wanted this clown to stay in one place while I asked him questions.

Outside, the turmoil gradually peaked and died down. No police showed up, and the crowd was comprised chiefly of whores and clients, none of whom were too keen on interfering in anything. I heard Suzette say something about filthy bleeding Russians, but I don't think anyone paid very much attention to her. When it all died down, Julia knocked softly on the door and I let her in.

"There were blanks in the gun," she said.

"You didn't know?"

"How would I have known? Lord, that was a wrench, wasn't it? Has my hair suddenly turned gray?"

"No."

"That's remarkable. I think he's coming awake, Evan."

He was indeed. His eyes went in turn to his bonds, to me, to Julia. He tried unsuccessfully to rock the chair. He looked at Julia again. "Effing little bitch," he said. "I thought you were too bloody good to be true."

I told Julia to take a taxi home. She told me not to be silly, that she was as anxious as I to hear what he had to say. I said that Nigel would worry about her, and she said that Nigel was at the theater.

"You may not enjoy this," I said.

"Oh, but I will, Evan."

What's-his-name looked up at me. "Evans, eh? And a good day to you, Mr. Evans." He didn't sound much upset. "Wha'd you shoot me with?"

"A blank."

"An effing blank." He laughed. "That's a good one. I'll remember that one, I will."

I pulled a card chair up and sat down in front of him. "You'll have to remember quite a few things. Your name, to start with."

"Wyndham-Jones, Mr. Evans."

"Not Smythe-Carson?"

"Who's he, Mr. Evans?"

I closed my eyes for a moment. Then I said, "There are some things you'll have to tell me. I'm not interested in you at all, just in your information. There was an American girl named Phaedra Harrow. You may have known her as Deborah Horowitz." I showed him her picture. "I want to know where she is and what's happened to her."

"Glad to oblige," he said cheerfully. "Let's have another look at the picture." His eyes narrowed in concentration. Then he smiled. "Don't know as I can help you, Mr. Evans. Never saw her before in me life, not the least bit familiar. Names don't ring a bell either, sorry to say."

I let him have the gun butt on his left cheekbone. His head flew to the side. I heard Julia suck in her breath, but He Who Got Slapped didn't make a sound. The smile came back and the same flat cold light glinted in his eyes. He said, "Two or three hours, I'll have a ruddy great bruise there. All blue and purple it'll be."

"The girl."

"Still don't know her, Mr. Evans. Me memory's no better."

I swung the gun backhand and caught him on the right cheekbone. I knew he'd ride with it, so I made it harder. "Now they'll match," I said.

"Oh, I'll be the pretty one."

"I can stand this longer than you can."

"Oh, can you now?" His lips tightened and his voice turned harder. "You effing bastard, I've taken dumpings from professionals. You haven't the stuff to kill me, and you'd have to do that to learn the first bloody thing about your little American twist. I'll sit here and take it while you puke at the horror of it all."

I hefted the gun. He didn't even wince. I stood up, turned to Julia. She was standing near the door and looked vulnerable. It was senseless. We had the son of a bitch tied up, and he was in control of the situation while Julia looked vulnerable and I felt impotent. I took a few deep breaths and concentrated on visions of a naked Phaedra being tortured and burned at the stake. I was trying to work up some genuine fury, and it just didn't come off. That sort of reaction either happens or it doesn't. You can't think it into existence.

So to Julia I said, "You see the problem? You pinpointed it earlier. I'm just not the menacing type. I don't ooze brutality. I've got a bad image."

"Evan—"

"Now if it was me in the chair and this clown asking the questions, he wouldn't have to lay a hand on me. One good glower from Hyphen here and I'd sing like a goddamned roomful of castrati." I thought for a moment. "Go home," I told her. "You don't want to see this."

"I'm not going anywhere."

"Go home. Now."

She shook her head.

"Horrible image," I mused. I left the room and wandered through the rest of the flat. I had wondered what sort of person would live in a whorehouse, and the other rooms answered the question for me. A whore lived there,

and Hyphen had borrowed her place for the evening.
There was female clothing in the closets, messy cosmetic
tubes and jars and bottles scattered in the bedroom and
bathroom. In the kitchen I fumbled through drawers until
I found something that was a sort of cross between a
regular knife and a meat cleaver. I think it's used for
chopping up heads of lettuce.

I got a roll of adhesive tape from the bathroom cabinet
and tore off eight or ten six-inch strips, fastening them
together to make a square patch. I returned to the front
room. He was as I had left him.

"Last chance," I said. He told me what to do to myself,
and I fastened the patch of tape over his mouth.

"What's that, Evan?"

"A gag. So he won't scream."

I bent a loose end of picture wire back and forth until
it frayed. The piece was long enough to wrap around the
index finger of his right hand five times, and while I was
doing that Julia asked me what it was.

"A tourniquet," I said.

"What is it for?"

"So he won't bleed when I cut off his finger. Go in the
other room, Julia. You don't have to go home if you don't
want to, but please get the hell out of here."

She went. I caught a glimpse of her face on the way
out. She looked slightly nauseous. I picked up the cleaver
and looked at Hyphen. For the first time his eyes had lost
that maddening assurance.

I said, "You think I'm bluffing but you're not certain.
You can gamble, but if you're wrong it'll cost you a
finger. Ready to talk?"

He nodded. I yanked the gag off. "Last chance," I said.
"Make it good."

"You'd cut off a bloke's finger."

"Yes."

"Undo that wire, mate. Me whole finger's throbbing."

"Talk."

He sighed heavily. "It's a fiddle I've got. A smuggling

fiddle, the birds do the smuggling. A perfect blanket, six lonely birds looking at bleeding tombs."

"Go on."

"I could do with a cigarette, mate."

"You could do without one. You took the girl along. Then what happened?"

His face clouded. "Bloody thing went bad. The peelers landed on us with both feet. All six girls wound up in the moan-and-wail."

"And you?"

"Bought me way out. Would have bought them out, but I hadn't enough of the ready."

"Where did this happen?"

"Turkey. Ankara. We brought guns in and would have brought gold out, but the bloody—"

I never found out what the last *bloody* was intended to modify, because I cut off the flow of words by slapping the tape back in place. I said, "You're very stupid. You don't know how much I know, so it's a bad time to try lying to me. You're a dreadful liar to begin with. It's just not your bag, and from now on you'll have to avoid it. This one particular lie just cost you a finger."

He struggled. His whole body went rigid, and for a moment I thought he might be strong enough to snap the wire. He wasn't.

I cut through the finger just above the second joint, about half an inch below the wire tourniquet. There was hardly any bleeding at all.

He did not turn his eyes aside. He watched his finger until I had succeeded in separating it from his hand, his face growing steadily paler, and then he quietly passed out.

"Just never expected it of you. The way you talk and all, and how you handle your face, and especially you being a Yank." His tone was soft and marveling, as if he had just witnessed something extraordinary on the telly. "You're all at once Lee Marvin in the bloody movies. An effing butcher working on a side of beef.

"I told you."

"Don't say you didn't, but Jesus effing Christ, you could have told me forever and I'd have gone on sending you up. You know what? Me finger hurts. Now why in hell should it do that? I mean it hurts where it was. Like the air hurts where me finger would be if you hadn't sliced it off. I wouldn't mind so much if it wasn't such an important finger. The little one on the left hand, say." He shook his head slowly from side to side. "Did you cosh me afterwards or did I do a faint?"

"You fainted."

"What I thought. Never did that before in me life. And you just sat there cool as ice."

"No. I went into the other room and was sick to my stomach."

"Did you? And if I don't talk now, or don't tell it straight, you'd do it again?"

"I'd do the thumb next."

He sighed again. "Not half hard, are you? And then?"

"Use your imagination. An eye, an ear, I don't know."

"Holy Bloody Mary. Imagine if the peelers bought your line. They'd never bring a lad in but he'd tell 'em anything they wanted to know. Be no staying out of jail then, would there? And imagine the poor bloody pickpockets with their hooks trimmed down like this. Be the end of crime, wouldn't it?"

He clucked at the wonder of it. Oh, it would be quite an innovation, I thought. It would return English criminal procedure to the days of the sixteenth century.

I said, "The girl."

"Oh, you'll get the whole of it now, mate. The fiddle's a sweet one. I worked it twice last year and once in the spring, and then in August with your bird. How it works, see, you try to attract the type of bird who's all alone in the world. They all of 'em come to London, you know. Maybe they've got a mother in Ireland that they don't even write to, or a maiden aunt up in Geordie country, or nobody at all. The others you send away, tell 'em the position's filled. You do the same with the dogs. They don't have to be beauties, you know, but they won't do if they're too fat or too thin or too old."

"Go on."

"Well, you get six or seven, see, just enough but not too many, and then you feed 'em a tale. The first time I made it that we were off to rob a tomb and everybody'd have a share in the plunder. Didn't go down as well as it might have. Oh, I filled my boat, you know, but some right ones shied away from it." He smiled suddenly. "Got the tale from the only other man who ever worked this fiddle, him that told me about it when we did a spell at Broadmoor together. And since then somebody put a flick in him, so I'm the only chap who knows it. Made up a better tale since then. I sort of worked in this espionage angle, James Bond and all, and—"

"I know the story."

"Oh, right, your bird told you. Well. I check 'em all out, see, and then I swear them all to secrecy. Nothing a bird likes better than being trusted with a secret, especially the lost and lonely ones that wouldn't know who to tell it to anyway. Once they're sworn to secrecy and once you've got the right crew, then you fly the lot of them to Istanbul. That's in Turkey."

"I know."

"Pack the lot of 'em into a Land Rover and just keep driving east. It's a grand time for them. You get girls who've never been out of London in their lives, or spent thirty years in a cottage in Cornwall, and here they're getting the grand tour. Turkey, Iraq, Persia. I don't rush 'em, I let 'em have their bit of sightseeing. And you just keep heading east until you get to Kabul. That's in—"

"Afghanistan."

"Right you are, Afghanistan. Never heard of the bloody country before me china put me onto this fiddle, let alone Ka-bloody-bul. Just drive straight on into it. There's some desperate roads on the way, and this last time I was carrying extra water the whole trip, what with the radiator boiling over, but that's the only problem there is. Crossing the borders is safe as houses, what with me own passport

in order and all of the birds' too. You have to make sure
of that ahead of time, that the birds have their passports
right, and the visas and all. Customs is no problem.
There's no smuggling, see, just the lot of birds."

"And then what?"

"And then there you are in Kabul."

I looked at him. I had the feeling I was missing a fairly
obvious point. He wasn't lying now. Somehow my act of
dedigitation had elevated me to the level of a man he
could respect, and he seemed to be telling me the details
of his fiddle with a pride akin to Courtney Bede's delight
in showing off his stacks of old newspapers.

"I don't understand," I said. "Do you have sex with the
girls?"

"With the birds?" He frowned, thinking. "I suppose a
chap could if he wanted. You'll get some who are proper
dying for it, but I never fool with any birds that way."

"Then what in hell do you do with them?"

"Oh, come on now," he said. "You're not half thick, are
you? Now you can work it out. Here you are in bloody
Kabul with six or seven girls, and what do you do?"

"I don't know."

"Why, you *sell* 'em, don't you see? What the hell else
would you do with them?"

I said, "You sell them."

"And to think you couldn't guess it! White slaves is
what they call it. And a thousand nicker each is what they
pay. That's six or seven thousand a trip, and add a bit of
profit on selling the Land Rover and take away the cost of
flying 'em to Turkey and you're still five or six thousand
quid ahead of the game. Just play it out four times a year,
say, and—"

"Wait a minute. You sell them. Who buys them?"

"Chap named Amanullah. A great hulking wog with
white hair to his shoulders. Never an argument on price,
not once."

"What happens to the girls?"

"They make brasses of them. Tarts. They've a shortage
of them over there, do you know?" He gave a short laugh.

"Fancy bringing a boatload of tarts to Soho and trying to sell 'em. Be coals to Newcastle all over again."

"They work in Kabul, then?"

He shrugged. "Got me there. I'd say they don't, now that I think on it. I'd say they ship 'em out where birds are scarce. For them that work in the mines and such. You know what? I never gave it much thought. Once I sell 'em they're nothing to me, and it's hop a plane and Hello, Picadilly! with a purse full of the ready."

I sat beside him, my mind quite numb, while he added details. I nodded at the right places, put in the right questions, and tried to convince myself that all of this was really happening. I glanced from time to time at his index finger on the floor. It looked like one of those plastic things they sell in novelty shops along with rubber dog shit and dribble glasses. It wasn't real, and neither was anything else.

He'd never had trouble with the girls until this last trip, he told me. Then two of them got wind of something, Phaedra and a farm girl from the Midlands, and in Baghdad he caught them trying to escape to the British Embassy. "Had to drug them and keep them in a fog the rest of the way. Told the others they were sick with a fever. Cost me a few quid that way, bribing the hacks at the borders. But the rest never did catch on."

I pumped him for more details about Amanullah and how he could be located. Finally it got through to him that I actually wanted to go to Afghanistan and get Phaedra back. I think this shocked him more than the loss of the finger. All along he had thought that I wanted to muscle in on his racket.

"You must be crackers," he said. "You'd never find her, and they'd never let you have her. She's been sold, don't you see? Oh, you might buy her back, but after a few months of that life, why, what would she be good for? They don't last long there, you see. That's why they've got a steady need for fresh birds—"

I thought of Phaedra, my little Phaedra, Mama Horowitz's Deborah. Sweet, virginal Phaedra, who lived with me for a month and emerged intact. It's not logical just to save yourself, I had told her once. You have to be saving yourself *for* something.

And what had my Phaedra saved herself for? A whorehouse in Afghanistan?

I stood up. Hyphen—I still didn't know his name, or much care—was saying something. I had stopped listening. I found the square of adhesive tape and slapped it in place across his horrible mouth.

Julia was in the bedroom. She was pressed up against the far wall, her arms across her chest, hugging herself and silently shaking. She looked like certain pictures of Anne Frank.

"Did you hear any of that?"

She nodded.

"I want you to go into the hallway now. I want to be certain that there's no one around when I walk out of here. Go out and close the door. I'll be ready in a moment or two, and I'll knock on the door. If it's all clear, return the knock and I'll come out."

She nodded again, rigidly, then grabbed up her purse and walked straight to the front room and out the door without looking at him. I went over to him and picked up the cleaver, but it was no good. I took it to the kitchen and exchanged it for a more pointed knife.

He didn't like the looks of it at all.

I spent a few unintentionally brutal seconds standing there trying to think of something to say, but there was no way to say it and no reason to try. So I put the knife in his heart, and took it out, and put it back a second time and left it there.

Chapter Four

❊ ❊ ❊

Afghanistan consists of a quarter of a million square miles of mountainous terrain bordered on the west by Iran, on the south and east by Pakistan, and on the north by the Turkmen, Uzbek and Tadzhik Soviet Socialist Republics. The population is slightly in excess of fifteen million, a thirtieth of whom live in greater Kabul. The monetary unit is the afghani. Major languages are Afghan and Persian. The chief religion is Islam. Camels and sheep constitute the most important livestock. There is some gold mined in the extreme northeast in the Hindu Kush, in which area is located the highest peak in the nation, which rises 24,556 feet above sea level. Substantial amounts of coal and iron are also to be found here and there. Major rivers include—

If you care, you might check out Hammond's Medallion Atlas, which was my own source for all of the above information. Nigel had a copy, and I divided my time that night between it and the coal fire, which was not throwing as much heat as I thought it should.

By midnight, both Nigel and Julia had gone off to bed. Our conversation until then was forced and uncomfortable. No one much wanted to discuss what had gone on at the Old Compton Street flat, and it was difficult to put one's mind to anything else, but we did make a pretense of talking over the barbarous notion of white slavery and the possible course of action I might take.

The former topic was limited to lines like, "Imagine that sort of thing in the twentieth century," and so on. I didn't find it all that hard to imagine, but then I'm not all that thrilled with the twentieth century, which may explain my feelings. The latter subject, just what to do about it, kept running into conversational dead ends. As far as I could see, there was only one thing to do. I had to go to Afghanistan, find Phaedra, and lead her Mosaically out of the house of bondage. I didn't imagine this would be a simple matter, but neither did I see how discussing it could render it a whit less difficult.

So they went to bed, and I read the atlas and poked at the fire and tried to figure out what the hell I was going to do.

I'd have saved a lot of time if it hadn't been for the silly atlas. But the more I concentrated on the precise geographical location of Afghanistan, the more elaborate plans I devised for working my way into the country. The best route, I finally decided, would constitute a close approximation of the course the girls themselves had followed. I'd have to omit Turkey, of course, where I am as *non grata* as a *persona* can possibly be. But other than that it wouldn't be too difficult to get into Iraq, then move on to Iran, then make the final crossing into Afghanistan.

Would Iraq be a problem? I wondered about this. The Kurds have been in armed rebellion against the Iraqi government for over twenty years, fighting incessantly and heroically for autonomy, and theirs is not the sort of struggle from which I am inclined to remain aloof. This might well limit my chances of obtaining an Iraqi visa. Still, that couldn't be too hard a border to cross, could it?

I studied maps.

This sort of thing went on for hours. I brewed fresh tea, added more coal to the fire (without adding more heat to the room), and wasted more time. I prepared for a variety of unlikely contingencies, none of which I'll bore you with now. My mind went on and on, never hitting upon the basic geometrical postulate that the shortest distance between two points is a straight line.

Blame it on my past. When one is sufficiently experienced in the devious, one rejects the straightforward approach as a matter of course. It took me hours and hours before I realized that the easiest way to go to Afghanistan was to go to Afghanistan.

Quite so.

No one in Afghanistan had anything to fear from me. It was one country where I was as welcome as any other stranger. Nor was there anything at all clandestine or subversive in my purpose for going there. I wanted to repurchase a slave and take her home, and I intended to do this quietly and discreetly, thus constituting not the slightest threat to the peace and stability of the Afghan nation.

So why not fly to Kabul?

I closed the atlas and returned it to its place on the shelf. There was probably an Afghan embassy or consulate somewhere in London. I could go to it in the morning and find out what I would need in the way of visas and inoculations. Any of the travel bureaus I had previously haunted could find a way to book me straight through to Kabul. A direct flight seemed too much to hope for, but no doubt there was a way to make connections through Teheran or Karachi or something. I wouldn't have any trouble flying out of England, either; my passport, with the entrance visa stamped at Dublin, was in good order. The British might have made it hard for me to enter their country, but my leaving it could only please them, if in fact, they took any particular note of it at all.

It was a few minutes past four when Julia screamed.

This wasn't the first time that sounds had come from behind her door. Periodically I had heard moans and groans, and while these did nothing for my concentration, they came as no great surprise to me. She was a fine girl, strong and resolute and bright, an echo of those superb

English girls who distinguished themselves during the blitz in movies of the Second World War. But it had been a hell of an evening, and the episodes of amateur surgery and murder were the sort that might disturb anyone's sleep.

I thought the scream would wake Nigel. It didn't. I walked slowly toward her door, listening for another cry. It didn't come, and I stayed with my ear to her door for a few minutes, but she seemed to be sleeping again. I went back to my fireside chair and sat down.

An hour later there were more moans. Then, a few minutes after that, her door opened and she appeared. She was wearing a shapeless robe the color of an army helmet. Her feet were bare.

"I can't sleep, Evan," she said. "I've been dreaming like a small child with indigestion. I must look frightful."

Her hair was snarled and her face drawn, but she looked remarkably fine in spite of this. I told her so, and she told me I lied superbly but she knew better. She went away and came back with her face washed and her hair combed and looked even better.

"I hope I'm not disturbing you?"

I said she wasn't, that I'd run out of things to read and had made all the necessary plans. She wanted to know about these, and I explained that I intended to go to Kabul by going to Kabul, which struck her as good sense all around. She drew up a chair and sat beside me near the fire. It wasn't doing very well. She studied it for a few moments, then rearranged a few coals with the poker. Flames leaped almost instantly.

"When I do that," I said, "nothing happens."

"You want practice. Tell me about her, Evan."

"Phaedra?"

"Yes. You must love her very much."

"I did."

"And don't you now?"

"I'm not sure."

"Were you lovers for very long?"

"We weren't lovers at all," I said. She looked at me

oddly, and I went on to explain the particular relationship Phaedra and I had shared. She found this revelation quite extraordinary. Then her face went positively gray.

"A virgin," she said. "And her first time must have been—"

"Yes. In Afghanistan."

"That's absolutely horrid. Defloration is dreadful under the best conditions, isn't it? My own first time—" she colored very slightly, then suddenly grinned. "Hear the girl go on and on! And see her blush with echoes of the old Victorianism. I don't really suppose you suspected I was a virgin, and it would be shameful if I were, wouldn't it? Yet one feels reluctant to abandon that little charade unless one is married. Do you know that I've never even discussed my affairs with Nigel?"

"That's not surprising."

"Then the surprise is that there's no surprise, because it *is* absurd, don't you think? We're closer than the average sister and brother, and I'm sure he knows I've had lovers, and neither of us has any moral objection to that sort of thing, God knows, and still I couldn't possibly discuss it with him. We sort of assume that I'm intact, and if I married we'd assume that I weren't. I don't want to be, actually."

"Intact? Or married?"

"Either. You've never married, have you, Evan?"

"No."

She looked into the fire. "Of course men marry later. I'm getting on to thirty, though, and one does feel one is missing something by not having children, and one can't very well have them without being married. I suppose one could, but—"

"I have two," I said. And then I found myself telling her about Todor and Jano, my two magnificent sons who live in the Macedonian hills with their mother, Annalya. I have seen Todor once; I bounced him upon my knee at the time that Jano was conceived. (Not the *precise* time, that would have been indecent, but that week.) I have not yet seen Jano, except in a charcoal sketch which some

IMRO patriots smuggled out of Yugoslavia and mailed to me. Todor looks like me. Jano thus far just looks like a baby.

"How remarkable," Julia said.

"Not really. Most babies—"

"No, no. That you compartmentalize your life the way you do."

I had never thought of it that way. The fire had died down again, and Julia crossed her arms over her breasts and gripped each elbow with the opposite hand. She had clutched herself thus in the bedroom on Old Compton Street, but there the chill had been emotional.

"It's so damned cold," she said. "I ought to be in bed but I can't sleep. When will you go to Kabul?"

I turned. "I don't know. As soon as I can. A day or two, I suppose."

"Yes."

"Depending on visas and—"

She stood up abruptly. "Could we make love, do you think?"

"Uh—"

"I hate being so awkward about it, but there's so little time." She was facing away from me. I looked at the khaki robe and imagined the body beneath it. "This ought to be romantic, and instead it's a damp morning with a dying fire and a memory of nightmares and death."

"Julia."

She turned to face me. "And I feel neither passionate nor in love, which is an awful thing to admit at such a moment, and I look a fright—"

"You're beautiful."

"—and perhaps it's obscene to use sex as therapy, but I do want to be in bed and I don't want to be alone, and I'm not saying this at all well, I know that. When I close my eyes I see that wretched man's finger. I never actually saw it, I rushed through there without looking at him, but with my eyes closed I see it dismembered and flapping about on the floor like a bisected angleworm. I shouldn't talk about this, it's as romantic as a stomach pump—"

I took her arm. "Be still," I said.

"Evan—"

I kissed her lips. She said, "I wish we were on a hill in Macedonia. In a little hut in the middle of nowhere eating charred lamb and drinking whatever they drink. I wish—"

"Don't talk."

"I wish I were ten years younger. Children take this sort of thing so much more casually. I wish I were either more or less emancipated. I—"

"Be quiet."

"All right."

Her room was small and dark, her bed narrow. We kissed with more love than passion. I felt the warmth of her flesh through her robe. I touched the belt of the robe and she stiffened. "Oh, damn," she said. "You mustn't look."

"What's the matter?"

"Oh," she said. "Oh it's so bloody unromantic. If you laugh I shan't blame you, but I'll never forgive you." With a defiant flourish she opened the robe. Beneath it she was wearing a one-piece suit of red flannel underwear. I didn't laugh. I just asked if the outfit had a drop seat.

"Damn you," she said.

I told her she would look pretty whatever she wore. She said it was bad enough that I was seeing her like this but that she couldn't let me watch her remove the garment. I turned around and got out of my clothes. By the time I had finished she was in bed beneath a mountain of quilts and blankets. I joined her, and we huddled together for warmth and love.

I held her close. She pressed her face to my throat while my hands stroked the smooth taut skin of her back and bottom. This, I knew, was what mattered—the warmth, the closeness. Whether or not we consummated the morning's entertainment was immaterial. There was no urgency to it, and might not be, and it hardly mattered.

"I won't be able to bear you a bonnie English bastard," she whispered. "I take the pill."

"Good."

"Wouldn't you care for an English bastard?"

"You talk too much."

"Silence me with a kiss."

And it was slow and thoughtful, a sweet sharing with little love and less passion and worlds of warmth and tenderness. Kisses both long and slow, and bits of whispered nonsense, and the comfortable touching of secret flesh.

A little at a time the world went away. The horror of Old Compton Street, the ice-eyed man in the chair, the wire wound round his finger, the sound of the cleaver parting flesh and bone. And the long knife, and his blenched face, and the knife going in and out and in again. All of this faded slowly, as did all the burden of time and place.

Until, in the manner of a surprise guest, passion came.

I touched and kissed her, and her breathing deepened and she clutched me with sweet urgency. A pulse pounded in my temples. She beamed, wide-eyed, and said, "How nice!" and closed her eyes and sighed. I kissed her. I felt her firm little breasts against my chest and her legs, the muscles now taut, against my own. I touched the moist warmth of her loins. She opened for me, and I rolled hungrily atop her, and she said, "Yes, yes," and we kissed again, and—

And a querulous voice said, "Julia! Evan! Where in hell is everyone?"

A few moments later, when our hearts started again, she whispered that it was Nigel. I knew this. She added that he was awake and in the kitchen. I knew that, too.

"We can't," she added.

Again she had put words to the obvious. Our mutual desire was like a tree that had spent a hundred years growing only to be cut down in its prime in an instant. I was still lying on top of her, and I ached with want for her, but—

He called our names again.

"Maybe he'll go back to sleep," I suggested.

"No. He sleeps like the dead, but once he's up he's up. Oh, it's light out."

"Wonderful."

"Damn," she said. I rolled reluctantly off her. We looked soulfully at each other. It occurs to me now that it was the sort of moment at which we might both have started laughing. This did not happen. For some reason neither of us could appreciate the basic humor of the situation.

"He mustn't know about us," she said.

"Shall I hide under the bed?"

"No, don't be silly. Oh, hell. Let me think. He won't come in now, not while he thinks I'm sleeping, but how on earth can you get from here to the kitchen without going through the door? Evan, I can't even think—"

We heard him stumbling around in the kitchen. He had given off calling us, evidently having decided that his sister was sleeping and that I had gone off somewhere. Julia jabbed a finger into my shoulder, then pointed at the window."

"There's an alley leading to the street behind," she whispered. "You could go through it and come round in front again. Say you'd gone for a walk."

"Without any clothes on?"

"Put them on first, silly head." I wondered why that hadn't occurred to me. I climbed over Julia, trying to touch her as little as possible, and sat on the edge of the bed putting clothes on. I couldn't find my undershorts. They were obviously there somewhere, but I couldn't find them.

"We'll get them later," Julia assured me. "When he's gone. There's a matinee today and an evening performance as well. We'll have some time together, Evan."

I was tying a shoe. I turned to ask a wordless question, and she grinned impishly. "Time to finish what we've started," she said. "I'm sure I'll never forgive Nigel for this, but you will forgive me, won't you, darling?"

I brushed her lips with mine, finished tying the shoe,

crossed to the window. The damn thing was stuck, and I was convinced I was making a hellish amount of noise. Just as I yanked it open the doorbell sounded.

I looked at Julia. She shrugged. "It's me," I said. "I raced around the block in excess of the speed of light and got back before I started."

She told me I was daft. The flat was on the first floor, which would have been a blessing if we were in the States. We weren't, though. I crouched on the sill, tensed myself to avoid a flowerbed, and dropped ten or twelve feet to the ground. I landed on my feet, which was not surprising, and I stayed on them, which was. Then I headed down the narrow alley to the street behind.

It was still raining. I made my way around the block, solemnly cursing Nigel for not having had the common decency to sleep another half hour. Of course, I thought, the doorbell would have awakened him in any event, but by then we might have at least finished.

I plodded dutifully through the rain. All things come round to him who will wait, I comforted myself. Nigel Stokes was going to give a matinee performance that afternoon, and so would his sister and I, and this time we wouldn't have an audience.

At the final corner, I stopped and drew a long breath. I needed some sort of story, obviously. I couldn't very well say I'd been out to get a morning paper, or Nigel might well ask why I hadn't brought it back with me. He might also wonder why I'd gone off without my jacket or umbrella. I thought for a moment and decided to tell him I'd spent the past few hours at an all-night café in Piccadilly. It had been clear when I left, I would say, and he could chide me for being a foolish American who didn't know that one had to carry a brollie rain or shine, since rain was always a danger, and I could laugh along with him, and—

And I rounded the corner, and the street was cluttered with police cars, and half the policemen in London were beating a path to Nigel's door.

Chapter Five

❃ ❃ ❃

I looked at all those policemen, and I turned around and walked back around the corner. It never occurred to me to wonder why they were there. I certainly hadn't expected them, but it was patently obvious that they had come for me, and that it was more than illegal entry that had brought them. I walked quietly round the corner and down the street and around another corner, and although it went right on raining I was no longer bothered by it. There but for the grace of coitus interruptus, thought I, go I, down the drain.

I offered a silent prayer of gratitude for Nigel's early rising and Julia's modesty. A brief prayer. After all, it was only decent that something went right for a change, and on balance I was still far behind. I was coatless and brollieless and wanted for murder by the most efficient police force in the free world. And I couldn't turn myself in and try to prove my innocence because I didn't happen to be innocent.

How much did they know? It was important to find this out before I did anything, and it was also important to get as far from London as possible before they spread the alarm. If they knew no more about me than that I had been a guest of Nigel and Julia Stokes, then I could leave the country more or less as planned. If they knew my

name and had a picture of me, then the plans were
useless. And new ones called for.

I took a bus to Portsmouth some seventy miles south-
west of London. The trip took two hours and I spent
them both with my face hidden in a morning newspaper.
There was nothing in the paper about me or Mr. Hyphen.
In Portsmouth I ate eggs and chips at a horrible café and
went to a movie house. I saw the last half of an old Doris
Day movie, a short on lobster trapping, a UPA cartoon, a
slew of commercials, coming attractions for something,
and the first half of the Doris Day movie. I stayed and
saw the last half over a second time in the hope that they
would change the ending this time through and let Rock
Hudson lay her, but they didn't and he didn't. After my
experiences with Phaedra and Julia, I was left with the
feeling that the movie was true to life.

I went to another café and had steak and chips and
some very bitter coffee, then found another cinema and
saw an Italian thing in which everyone laid everyone else
but no one enjoyed it much. Least of all the audience.
When it ended I wasn't hungry, so I went straight on to
another theater and saw an English film based on the
Great Train Robbery. The police were magnificently
efficient in the film and everyone got caught at the end, so
this one did even less for my morale than the other two. I
was beginning to worry that Portsmouth might run out of
movies before I ran out of spare time, but the third movie
was the charm; when I left the theater the evening papers
were on the street. I bought both of the London dailies,
and they both had what I was looking for. One called it
MULTILATION AND MURDER IN SOHO SIN FLAT. The other
said AMERICAN SOUGHT IN SOHO TORTURE SLAYING. Aside
from that, they both told about the same story. They both
spelled my name right, and they both used the same
photograph over it.

I read them in the lavatory of a side-street pub. They
did not make me very happy. It was all my own fault, of
course. I had left fingerprints all over the murder flat,
mainly because it never occurred to me not to. I didn't

suspect that the English authorities would have my prints on file. Evidently they had obtained them a while back from Washington, because the body of Arthur Hook had not been discovered until shortly after midnight, and they could hardly have run a check through Washington that quickly.

It was fingerprints that put them onto me, but it was the two useless guns that told them where to look for me. The police identified them as theatrical props, routed people out of bed to check out various prop departments, and had them connected to Nigel in no time at all. I was beginning to appreciate why Scotland Yard enjoyed its extraordinary reputation. But not even the best police force on earth can cope with dumb luck, which was why I was in Portsmouth instead of jail.

Someone knocked on the lavatory door. I grunted inarticulately and went on reading. According to both articles, I was a Jacobite fanatic and known terrorist, and a variety of odd theories were advanced as probable explanations of my connection with Arthur Hook (alias Smythe-Carson, alias Wyndham-Jones). He had an interesting criminal record and I'm sure no one much regretted his death, but this didn't mean they weren't interested in getting their hands on his killer. All air and sea ports were being watched, all ticket offices had been circularized. Special attention was being paid to the Scottish border in view of my Jacobite connections.

This last bothered me. If I was going to get out of England, I was going to need help, and other members of the Jacobite League seemed like my best chance. They share my hope of chasing Betty Battenberg off the throne and restoring the venerable House of Stuart. There were any number of loyal men in the Scottish Highlands who would have sheltered me, but it looked as though that was precisely where the Yard would look first.

Another knock at the door. I folded the papers, grunted again, gave the loo an unnecessary flush, and sidled out of the door to keep the room's new occupant from seeing my face. It was wasted effort; he was far more interested in the room than in its previous tenant, and I walked on through the pub and out into the street.

The Jacobites were out, I decided. And now that Nigel had been picked up, the Flat-Earth people might well be under surveillance. Even if this weren't the case, I couldn't quite see running to them now. A man has to be something of a nonconformist to uphold the theory that the earth is flat, but this does not imply his readiness to grant sanctuary to a murderer.

I had to find some political extremists, and I had to go somewhere close, and I had to deal with people who were in the habit of traveling from one country to another without going through customs. Of course I could use my passport once I was well out of England, but—

The hell I could. It was in my jacket pocket, and my jacket, when last seen, was in Nigel's living room.

I found another pub. There were only a few drinkers in it, and none of them had newspapers. I ordered a double scotch and a pint of bitter, remembering to put on an Irish accent. People almost always hear discrepancies between one's speech and their own, so the trick is to give them an alternative set of discrepancies. If I had tried an approximation of the local speech I would have sounded American. This way I merely sounded Irish, which was unusual enough to be noticed but not likely to be long remembered.

I thought of trying some IRA friends. I knew some names and addresses in Liverpool and one in Manchester, plus any number in Ireland. But Ireland was an ocean away, and the few in England were still a good distance from Portsmouth.

Oh, of course. The CSU.

While auto theft is not as exclusively American a crime as kidnaping, it remains generally rare in England. Even in London few drivers take the trouble to lock their cars, and outside of the major cities it's common practice to leave keys in the ignition. I hate to lower someone's high opinion of human nature, but it was that or risk a bus or train, so I wandered through Portsmouth until I found a Morris 1000 with the key in it and no one watching it.

This was less than a miracle. The remarkable thing was that the car had over half a tank of gas, more than enough to get me to Cornwall. After the extravagance of movies and drinks, I had only eight or nine shillings left. My money belt still held a thousand dollars, but the idea of attempting to change an American fifty-dollar bill at a petrol station left me colder than the rain, which was still falling and which the windshield wipers of the Morris were having a tough time with.

Minor problem, that. I kept my hands on the wheel and my foot on the gas, and the Morris, while not a good car, was a good enough car, and on we went. Cosham, Southampton, Dorchester, Honiton, Exeter, Okehampton, Launceston, Bodmin, Fraddon, and Truro. And just past Truro, at the end of a lonely ill-paved road, the thatched cottage where lived Arthur Poldexter, corresponding secretary of the Cornish chapter of the Celtic-Speaking Union.

I don't suppose you've ever heard of the Celtic-Speaking Union. Not many people have. The organization came into being just a few years ago, spurred largely by the parliamentary success of Welsh and Scottish Nationalists and the concommitant interest in linguistic nationalism. The CSU is a five-branched nationalist movement aimed at joining in a loose political federation those geographical areas where Celtic languages prevailed longest. The five areas are Ireland, Scotland, Wales, Cornwall, and the French province of Brittany.

It would probably be infinitely easier to repeal the Law of Gravity than to transform the Celtic-Speaking Union into a political reality. This is nowhere more demonstrably the case than in Cornwall, where the old Celtic language of Cornish ceased to exist well over a century ago. As far as I was concerned, this only made the efforts of Arthur Poldexter and his fellows all the more admirable. Two of them, Ardel Tresillian and George Pollifax, had worked up a painstaking reconstruction of the Cornish language; I own a mimeographed copy of their manual and will study it as soon as I find the time.

I parked the Morris at the end of the lane and walked along a winding flagstone path, wishing as I walked that I had taken the time to learn Cornish properly. I knew just two words, and when the door opened to my knock I used them. "Free Cornwall!" I said.

Arthur Poldexter's black eyes flashed in his ruddy face. He had no idea who I might be or what I might want, but I was a Cornish speaker and that was all that mattered. He gripped my shoulders, pulled me inside, and launched a flood of words at me.

I didn't understand any of them.

"You must go to France, Evan. To Brittany—that would be best. The French police cooperate with the British, but there are comrades of ours among the Breton peasantry. I know several, and Pendennis and Trelease know others, and for sure you've friends there yourself. We should hide you here as long as you wish, but this evil land's no sanctuary for you. What we know as an act of political assassination those in power call a murder. It must be Brittany for you, Evan."

We had switched to English. Poldexter spoke a strongly accented English, but he was an educated man and was thus easier to follow than many of the locals might have been. He had not seen the newspapers yet. I gave him a version of the circumstances that was closer to the official story than the truth, figuring that the Jacobite League would get more of a response from him than some nonsense about white slavery in Afghanistan. He was instantly sympathetic and anxious to provide shelter. He went out to park the car where it would not be seen, and his little birdlike wife dished out a bowl of lamb stew and poured a huge mug of good brown ale for me.

"I'll be making inquiries," he assured me. "It's a smuggler's coast, this one. We're few of us in the movement, but every man has friends, and friends in this part of the world know when to ask questions and when to be still.

There's some I know that make night time voyages to the French coast, and what they take across is not what they bring back. Round Dover, now, is where the crossing's easiest and the smuggling thickest. There 'tis twenty mile across, and here nearer a hundred mile, but then at Dover the officials keep a keener watch. We'll lay a bed for you now and you'll sleep the night, and in the morning will we see what's to be done for you."

It was easier to let his wife make up a bed beside the fire than to explain why I didn't need one. I nursed a jar of ale until sunrise. Arthur Poldexter left after breakfast, first furnishing me with his files of correspondence so that I might jot down some contacts in Brittany.

I didn't bother doing this—once across the Channel I could manage on my own—but I did get involved in the correspondence. The Celtic-Speaking Union seemed to be stronger in Brittany than I had realized. I was still reading when he returned.

He brought good news and bad. The bad was in the morning paper, a copy of the *Times* with a story which made it obvious that the authorities were extremely interested in capturing me, and that both Nigel and Julia had been taken into custody. I felt bad about involving them and only hoped they would have the sense to throw all the blame upon me.

But the bad news was predictable, and the good news was enough to offset it. A man named Trefallis or something like that knew a man who knew a man who was taking a midnight run to France that very night. The ship would leave Torquay in Devonshire after sunset and would arrive somewhere near Cherbourg before dawn. They would want money, he told me. Perhaps as much as thirty pounds. Had I that sum?

"In American dollars," I said. "But it might be better if they didn't know I was American."

"It would be better if they knew nought of you. I've a friend who would change your dollars, but you'd lose some on the exchange."

Thirty pounds comes to seventy-two dollars. I gave

Poldexter two fifties, figuring that even heavy robbery on
the exchange wouldn't net me less than thirty pounds. He
came back with forty pounds and ten shillings and an
apology, telling me sadly that I should be receiving another pound, three more shillings, and fourpence, or a hot
$2.80. You can't do better than that at a bank.

It was a clear day, with fair weather forecast through
the following afternoon. I passed the afternoon walking in
the fields. It was beautiful country, rugged and windswept
and raw, and at a better time I would have enjoyed myself
greatly. But there were too many things on my mind.

After dinner I played at altering my appearance, but
there wasn't very much I could do. The Scotland Yard
photo had been taken when my hair was shorter than it
was presently, so cutting it was purposeless. Nor was there
time to grow a beard or moustache. I confined my efforts
to making myself look less American. I lengthened my
sideburns a half-inch with charcoal and changed my own
clothes for some of yet another friend of my hosts whose
name I don't remember except that it began with Pol or
Pen or Tre, as did they all—*By Pol and Tre and Pen/Ye
may know the Cornish men*, as the old rhyme has it. I
wound up with a heavy tweed jacket patched at the elbows and a rubberized mackintosh. And I played with my
facial expression and worked on my brogue; I would be a
Liverpudlian running out on a forgery charge, if anyone
wanted to know.

By seven-thirty it was time to leave. A lad named
Pensomething was driving me to Torquay in his father's
Vauxhall, and Poldexter had arranged to keep my stolen
Morris until someone needed a ride to London, where it
could be safely abandoned. We said our good-byes all
around, toasted Free Cornwall as an equal partner in the
Celtic-Speaking Union, and away I went. The Vauxhall
was even worse than the Morris but at least I didn't have
to drive it.

I don't know much about boats. The one I boarded at
Torquay was about twenty feet long and it had a down-

stairs and an upstairs which I know aren't called that. I guess you call them "topside" and "below," but I wouldn't swear to it. I really don't know much about boats beyond the fact that it's better to be on them than in the water. I also know that starboard is the right and port is the left, unless it's the other way around.

Fortunately I didn't really have to know much. I bargained with the captain and wound up paying twenty-five pounds for my passage, which was five less than I'd anticipated. Then I got on board and found a nice quiet corner and pretended to go to sleep. More men got aboard, and some of them loaded crates of something into the downstairs part of the ship, call it what you will. I went on pretending to be asleep, and I kept up this pretense until we were well under way, at which point it became impossible to go on because sleeping men do not vomit, and I had to.

One other thing I know about boats—if you have to throw up, you don't do it into the wind. I threw up correctly and felt quite proud of myself. I was standing at the rail feeling proud of myself when a thin dark man with a spade-shaped beard came over and stood beside me. "You are not so much of a sailor," he said dolefully.

"I picked the right side," I said.

"How is this?"

"I didn't puke into the wind," I said. "I went to the port side and—"

"But this is the starboard side."

"Precisely," I said.

I escaped from him, regained my quiet corner and wrapped my mackintosh around me. It wasn't raining but it might as well have been, because the Channel was choppy and there was enough of a wind to keep an icy spray zinging over the deck. For this I had left October in New York.

I heard footsteps approaching and forced myself not to look up. The steps ceased. Beside me, a man cleared his throat laboriously. I ignored this, but he was not a man to be ignored. He sat down on the deck beside me and put a hand on my shoulder.

"You," he said.

I made a pretense of coming groggily awake. I blinked at him. He was a young giant with shaggy blond hair beneath a black beret. His face was a mass of amorphous dough, almost featureless, marked by diagonal scars on both cheeks.

"Ho," he grunted. "You sick, hah? You want cup soup? Hah?"

I thanked him but explained that I didn't want a cup of soup just now.

"Tsigarette?"

Not that either, I said. Nothing just now, but thanks all the same.

"Is bad sea. Not to worry that you sick."

His accent was hard to place. There was a Baltic undertone to it, and if I'd had to guess I'd have labelled him Finnish or Estonian.

"You American?"

"Irish," I said.

"Irish. Hah."

He went away. An odd crew, I decided. One expects smugglers to be natives of the port from which they operate. On the south coast of England and the Isle of Wight, smuggling has long been a family occupation, with the tricks of the trade passed down from father to son over the centuries. It seemed odd that this particular smuggler would have put together a crew of foreigners. The Baltic giant was no native of Devon, nor was the dark man with the spade-shaped beard, who, now that I thought about it, had a definite flavor of Eastern Europe in his voice.

Time passed slowly. Most of the men were downstairs, and I was torn between a desire to join them—obviously it would be warmer there, with the wind less of a factor— and the stronger desire to stay by myself. The channel crossing was something like eighty miles, and I had no idea how long it was going to take. The boat did seem to be traveling at a good pace, but I had no idea what that might mean in knots—or what knots meant in real miles per hour.

I suppose we were halfway across when the Irishman sat down next to me.

"I'm told you're a kinsman of mine," he said. "Where are ye from?"

I looked at him. I couldn't place his accent. "Then you're Irish yourself," I said.

"I am."

That was no help. I said something about Liverpool.

"And you're after saying good-day to Mother England, are ye?" •

"I am that."

"Not one of those IRA lunatics, I hope."

"Oh, hardly that," I said. "It seems I wrote a check and put some other lad's name on the bottom of it, do you see?"

He laughed and slapped me on the shoulder. He told me his name was John Daly, and that his home was in County Mayo, and he'd spent some good days in Liverpool. Just where did I live in Liverpool? And did I know this chap, and that chap, and —

Someone called him about then, and he slapped me on the back again. "More bloody orders," he said. "What you get when you take up with foreigners. They won't keep me long, and I've a bit of holy water I'll bring with me when I can. We'll have ourselves a few jars and talk about the old place, shall we?"

"Ah, God save ye," I said, or something like that.

And God help me, I thought. Something rather odd was going on and I seemed to be somewhere in the middle of it, along with being somewhere in the middle of the English Channel. I wondered whether he believed I was Irish or whether he was playing along with me. I wondered if we would ever get to France. I wondered why the crew was composed of so many foreigners. I wondered whatever had prompted me to leave New York.

A little while later I found out. The foreigners weren't members of the crew.

They were the cargo.

I was feigning sleep again when I got the message. Evidently my act was a good one, because a trio of men in leather jackets passed me without notice and stood talking at the rail. The group did not include any of the men I had previously spoken to. With the steady roar of the wind, I could not at first make out any of what they were saying, but they did not sound English. Then the wind died down a bit, and it became evident that the reason they did not sound English is that they were speaking Russian.

I caught a few words here, a few words there. They were talking about guns and supplies and explosives and revolution. I listened intently while the wind blew up and died down, blew up and died down again. It was extremely frustrating. My Russian is fluent, but with the noise the wind was making I would have had trouble understanding them whatever language they spoke. On top of that they seemed to be speaking a dialect of Russian with which I was not familiar, so that of those words which were intelligible there were some I had trouble understanding.

Still, I got the gist of it. They were on their way to some country where the groundwork was already being laid for a revolution.

They were set to overthrow a government.

When they went away, leaving me with no idea of just what government they were overthrowing, or when, or why, I pulled the mackintosh over my head and thought about frying pans and fires. It occurred to me that all of this was some extraordinarily involved put-on concocted for my benefit. This was a tempting theory, and in a way it made as much sense as anything else. Because why on earth would a batch of Russian agents be sneaking across the English Channel in a smuggler's boat? And what government were they going to overthrow?

"Ah, there ye are!" It was Daly, my Irish friend, with a

leather-covered flask in his hand. He sat cross-legged beside me, opened the flask, and took a long drink. "Bedad, there's no better remedy for the cold."

He sighed and passed the flask to me. *"Slàinte,"* I said, and drank. It wasn't just what my stomach had in mind, but by now I was used to the roll of the sea. Besides, the hell with what my stomach had in mind. A good draught of Irish whiskey was certainly what my mind had in mind, and right now that seemed the most important consideration.

He said, "Bloody Rooshians and Ukrahoonians and God knows what-all." He took another drink and passed the flask to me again. I drank. "The lads ye have to work with in this bloody business. A couple of fine boys like you and myself, there should be a better place for us than this slogging old tub and this mucking ocean. Sure, and half an hour more and we'll be in France."

"A long way from County Mayo," I said.

"Too far to walk, eh?" We laughed, and he had a drink and I had a drink. "Oh, a good long walk from County Mayo, and more than a hop skip jump from Liverpool, too. But France is still a damn sight closer to home than Afghanistan, I'd say."

I went numb. I said, "How did you know I was going to Afghanistan?"

He looked at me, and I looked at him, and that went on for longer than was entirely comfortable. "Bejasus," he said finally. "Then you're for it, too, are ye?"

"Uh—"

"Those bloody Rooshians. Here we are like McGinnis and McCarthy, two Irishmen in on the same show and neither bloody one knows that the other one's there. Do ye believe it now? Have ye ever heard its like?"

Oh, I thought, stupidly. He hadn't meant that Afghanistan was a long ways from Ireland for me to be. He had meant it was a long ways from Ireland for *him* to be. Which meant that he and the bloody Rooshians were on their way to just that spot, which in turn meant that I suddenly knew what government it was that they intended to overthrow. And which also meant, now that I had opened my idiot mouth, that he thought I was a part of the group, bound for the same destination with the same purpose, and—

Oh.

"And here's everyone saying you're only a paying guest the captain was greedy enough to take on, and you not knowing about us or we about you. Why, I'll let them know how things stand."

"No, don't do that."

"What, and contend with these foreigners meself? Let the bleeders know from the start they've two Irish lads to deal with."

"Have another drink first," I suggested.

"Have it for me," he said, passing me the flask. "I won't be a minute."

I took a long drink, shuddered, capped the flask. I had made a grave mistake, but now that I thought about it I could see how it might work out for the best. If they were really a crew of spies and saboteurs en route to Afghanistan, and if they were fool enough to accept me as one of their own, things might be infinitely easier. I could forget about the headaches of border-hopping. I'd just tag along with them, and when the whole bunch of us got to Afghanistan I could slip away and find Phaedra while they were busy billing and couping. I didn't know very much about the government of Afghanistan, but I've long felt that most governments are better overthrown, and if they put up with slavery, that makes them even better candidates for a coup d'etat. So if my shipmates would get me into the country, they were then welcome to do as they pleased with it.

I had another drink, a long one, and by the time Daly came back with four of his friends in tow, I was feeling positively giddy.

"So we're all of us bound for Afghanistan," I said. "Fancy that."

"No one tells us of you," the bearded one said.

"Nor I of you, for that matter. I received my instructions, how to cross the Channel and where to go. I thought I was to meet up with you on the other side."

"Where?"

"I was to receive further instructions at a drop in Cherbourg."

They looked at each other. "From whom did you receive orders?"

"A man called Jonquil. I do not know his actual name."

"Which section are you?"

"Section Eight," I said.

"You are in Section Eight and you were assigned to this operation?"

"I was requisitioned for it. Through Section Three."

"Ah, that has more sense to it." Thank heavens for that, I thought. "But this is most remarkable." The man with the spade-shaped beard turned to a chunky man with a bald head and cheap false teeth. "Get Yaakov," he said, in Russian.

"He sleeps."

"He has slept since he boarded this garbage scow. Wake him."

"He will be displeased."

"Tell him such are the penalties of leadership." He turned to me. I looked blank. In English he asked me if I spoke Russian. I told him I did not, and he told me that Yaakov, the leader of the expedition, would come to have a look at me. While we waited, we chatted pleasantly about the wind and the condition of the sea. The crossing was slower than anticipated, I was told, but in another fifteen minutes we should be reaching shore. I looked for France out ahead of the boat, but I could see nothing but inky blackness.

And then Yaakov made his appearance.

He didn't look as though he was in charge of anything. What he really looked like was Woody Allen, small and skinny and ineffectual. He peered myopically at me through thick horn-rimmed glasses, while the man with the beard explained in Russian who I was and what I was doing there.

Yaakov asked if I spoke Russian. I looked as blank as ever, and the bearded man said I didn't. Yaakov nodded, fastened his eyes on me again, and smiled shyly.

I returned the smile.

In Russian he said, "You are all fools. This man is not Irish but American. His name is Evan Tanner, he is an assassin who killed a man in London. He is not one of us at all. He is a spy and an assassin." He was still smiling the same shy smile, and his voice was very gentle. "I am going below now," he went on. "I will not be disturbed again until we reach the shore. Have the sense to kill this man and throw him overboard."

They were all looking at me. My friend Daly had evidently not understood the speech. The others had, however. Their faces showed that they had altered their opinions of me.

So I spun to my right and bellowed, *"Man overboard!"*

They turned to look. I shrugged my mackintosh off my shoulders and looped it over the head and shoulders of the man immediately to my left. While he was clawing at it I dodged around him and raced for the rail. I had time for another fleeting thought of frying pans and fires, and then I vaulted the rail, and then I was in the water.

Chapter Six

❀ ❀ ❀

The water permanently dispelled thoughts of frying pans and fires. If it had been any colder I could have played hockey on it. I left the rail in a lifesaver's jump, body bent forward, legs apart, arms wide, but at the last moment I must have done something wrong, because instead of staying above water I sank like a brick. Eventually my brain sent a night letter to my arms and legs and I made furious scrambling motions while waiting for my whole life to pass before me. I guess that only happens if you really drown. I broke the surface and breathed out and in a few times, and then I heard shouts and saw a spotlight swing laboriously around toward me. I drew a last breath and went under again just as the first bullets began slapping at the water's surface.

I tried swimming underwater, which is something I don't do awfully well under optimum conditions, which these clearly weren't. I surfaced and dove again before they could bring the guns around. Movement was very difficult, and at last I realized that it was my clothes which were causing the difficulty. But I'll be cold without them, I thought. Then it occurred to me that they were doing nothing to keep me warm underwater.

Years ago, when I took a lifeguard course, they taught us to strip completely before entering the water. It only takes a few seconds on land and you more than make up

for it in improved swimming speed. But I hadn't had the
time to spare when I left the ship. Now I worked my way
out of jacket and shirt, kicked off shoes and socks, ripped
open a stuck zipper and squirmed out of trousers. I would
have left my undershorts on—they can't slow one down
much, certainly—but I hadn't had them on to begin with.
As far as I knew they remained in Julia's room in London. So I swam on without them and worried about
sharks.

The sharks in the boat were a more immediate source
of danger. They must have circled for half an hour,
playing that damned spotlight over the water and popping
away with their guns in my approximate direction. As far
as I know, none of their shots came particularly close. It
was pitch dark out, I was underwater more often than
not, and the sea was sufficiently choppy to make observa-
tion tricky, not to mention marksmanship. After maybe
thirty minutes of this I guess they decided that if I hadn't
drowned already I would sooner or later. They stopped
circling and went rapidly away. I treaded water for awhile
until I couldn't hear their engines any longer. Then I
closed my eyes, and some of the more recent moments in
my life passed before me, and drowning, now that I
thought about it, seemed like a pretty good idea.

Virgins, white-slavers, smugglers, spies. I sighed heavily. The waves rolled on, as waves are apt to do. I remembered which way the boat had gone and pointed myself in
that general direction and set out to swim the English
Channel.

It took forever. I used to swim a lot years ago, and they
do say it's one thing you never forget, and evidently I
hadn't. Even so I kept expecting my strength to give out,
and I figured that sooner or later a wave would spill me
under the surface and I wouldn't have anything left to
pull myself back up again with. But I kept on going. The
water didn't get any warmer, but I stopped feeling it
before long.

Until finally there was a point when I knew I was going

to make it. The waves were going the same way I was, which helped immeasurably. Whenever I got sufficiently exhausted I could roll over on my back and float for a while. It wasn't quite as restful as a few hours in a hammock, but it helped.

I went off course, which was predictable but less than helpful. I missed the little peninsula that Cherbourg is at the tip of, and I suppose that must have cost me a couple of extra hours in the water. And when I did wash up on shore a few hours after sunrise there were some people on the beach. I staggered onto dry land, calling to them in French, and a woman shrieked, "Howard, he's naked as a jaybird!" and Howard aimed his Instamatic at me and took my picture.

Howard, it turned out, had washed up on this very spot almost twenty-five years ago in June of 1944. He was part of the Normandy invasion, and my channel swim had somehow deposited me on Omaha Beach. He said he wanted to bring the wife and have a look at the spot and to hell with what the President said about the gold shortage. His wife, eyes averted, said I would catch my death of cold, a possibility which had already occurred to me.

My skin was more blue than not and my teeth were doing their castanet number. Worse than that, I was lightheaded almost to the point of delirium. If they had asked me anything at all I would have told them some thoughtless approximation of the truth, and I suppose they would have either run away from me or turned me in.

But they never asked. Only American tourists could have been capable of such a feat. It was not reserve that prevented them from asking. I've thought about it for some time, and I can only conclude that they didn't ask because they didn't care. Howard wanted to talk about the Normandy invasion and the way the French girls welcomed them at the liberation of Paris. Howard's wife— I've forgotten her name—babbled intermittently about their wisdom in bringing rolls of American toilet paper with them.

Not that they ignored me. Howard found a terrycloth

bathrobe in the trunk of the car that they were buying in
Europe at a great savings, and I dried myself with it,
thinking it was a towel, and then, realizing my mistake,
put it on. This enabled Howard's wife to look at me.
Before I had been somewhat less naked than a jaybird—I
was still wearing my moneybelt around my middle—but
I'd still been distinctly exposed.

They made coffee for me. They had a thermos of hot
water, and Howard's wife had brought not only toilet
paper but a small jar of genuine American instant coffee.
They offered me a ride back to Paris, but I just couldn't
believe that I could spend that much time with them
without something going wildly wrong. It also occurred to
me that this might be a trap, that they would take me to
Paris only to turn me in at the American Embassy. This, I
told myself, was nonsense. But if my mind was capable of
such fantasies it only proved that I needed a few hours of
rest before making any major decisions. I rode as far as
Caen, with Howard continuing his monologue on the fun-
damental superiority of the American fighting man.
Howard's wife said "yes, dear" a lot, and when Howard
ran out of gas—figuratively, not literally, thank the saints—
she told me that they were from Centralia, Illinois. I said
that I had an aunt in Centralia, Washington. I don't know
why I said this. It isn't true. Howard's wife said that the
two cities were often confused, and that on occasion their
mail had been sent to Centralia, Washington by mistake. I
said that my aunt had often spoken of the same problem.

I left them on the outskirts of Caen. "Now I'm not
about to take that robe away from you," Howard said.
"Can't go doing that, even if this is France and all."

Howard's wife said, "Oh, Howie!" and giggled.

"So I'll just give you my card," he went on, "and you
send the robe back when you're done with it."

I wonder if he ever got the robe back. I left it in one of
the outbuildings of an apple orchard outside of Caen. The
hired men lived in the building, and they were all out
picking apples when I got there, so I went from bed to

bed until I found a set of clothes my size—corduroy button-fly trousers, a thick flannel shirt. From beneath another bunk I liberated two heavy white wool socks and a pair of ankle-length cordovan boots with steel reinforced toes. I gave them the terry cloth robe in return and left Howard's card in the pocket just in case they wanted to send it back to him.

It was nice to be wearing underwear again.

Under an apple tree in a neighboring orchard I stretched out on my back and let the world calm down. It was a clear and warm day, and gradually the heat baked the chill out of me. I had come as close as I ever would to an old boyhood dream of swimming the English Channel. I was alive, I was dry, and I was almost warm. I had clothes on my back and boots on my feet and nine hundred dollars around my waist.

So much for assets. I didn't even want to think about the other side of the ledger. I just wanted to get back to the States.

Yeah.

Well, what the hell else could I do? I couldn't fly to Kabul as planned, because those clowns who were planning to overthrow the government of Afghanistan would welcome me with open guns. I couldn't fly anywhere because I didn't have a passport. If the police picked me up, they would send me to England, and the English would put a rope around my neck. And—

Phaedra, I told myself. Sweet innocent Phaedra Harrow. Or Debbie Horowitz, as you prefer. Think about Phaedra.

Oh, the hell with her. I did what I could, and—

But I had killed a man on her account, hadn't I? Not that it had done her worlds of good, because the poor kid was chained up in some sort of Afghan whorehouse getting raped twenty or thirty times a day, and—

Good, I thought wickedly. She deserves it.

I sat up, clambered to my feet. I can't take too much credit for the decision to press onward. I'd like to attribute it entirely to concern for Phaedra and strength of moral fiber, but I've got to admit that there was more to it than that. Because, after all, it couldn't be too much harder for me to get to Afghanistan than back to New York. Either way I didn't have a passport. Either way I was wanted by the British for murder, and the U.S. would be more likely to extradite me. Either way I was in all kinds of trouble, and it's no great trick to be a hero when it doesn't cost you anything.

I hitchhiked to Paris. Everyone has friends in Paris, and I have some particularly useful ones. A family of Algerian colons fed me and wined me, and a friend of theirs drove me through town in a dented Citroen to the home of his old OAS comrade who lived in the attic of a decrepit tenement off the Boulevard Raspail in Montparnasse. The old comrade was in no shape to win a beauty contest— he'd lost a hand and most of his face when some *plastique* went off ahead of schedule. But he took five of my hundred-dollar bills and disappeared into the night, and when he'd been gone almost three hours I looked accusingly at the Citroen's driver.

"It is said by all that Léon is a trustworthy man," he said.

I said nothing.

"And yet five hundred U.S. is a great sum of money. Twenty-five hundred francs, is it not?"

I admitted that it was.

"One should not leave one's lambs in the care of too hungry a dog."

I agreed that one probably shouldn't.

"So we shall wait," my driver said, "and we shall see."

Léon was back before sunrise with a Belgian passport in the name of Paul Mornay. M. Mornay was fifty-three years old, stood five feet five inches tall, and weighed 214 pounds. They didn't even come right out and say this, either. It was all in centimeters and kilograms and such and I had to work it out in order to see just how far apart were M. Mornay and I. His picture was as far off the mark as his vital statistics. He had a round face and a

baldish head and a cute little moustache, and he looked
more like Porky Pig than Evan Tanner.

"It is genuine," Léon said.

"And M. Mornay?"

"M. Mornay has taken to bed one of the most energetic
tarts in Montmartre."

"From his picture," I said, "one would think it would
kill him."

"And so it did," Léon agreed. "At the critical moment, zut! The little death becomes the great one. Thus
did his passport come upon the market, and thus one may
rest assured that M. Mornay will not report its loss."

My driver said, "If one must die, no way is sweeter."
And, in the car, he said, "I must apologize for Léon. I
thought he was a trustworthy man."

"He brought the passport."

"If he paid more than a thousand francs for that passport then I am the bastard son of Enzo Ferrari and
Queen Marie of Rumania. For twenty-five hundred francs
one should obtain a U.S. or British passport in good
order, not a shabby Belgian thing that requires further
attention. One expects that Léon shall make a profit, but
this is larcenous."

"I didn't think he would come back at all."

"Ah," said my driver. "But did I not assure you he was
a trustworthy man?"

My barber was also a trustworthy man. He was one of
the few White Russians in Paris who didn't insist he had
been a prince before the revolution. He said he had been a
barber, and he was a barber still. His craft was only
slightly impaired by the tremor which age had put in his
fingers. He agreed that it was sensible to doctor me rather
than the passport insofar as possible. He shaved me, leaving a moustache to match M. Mornay's and he showed me
how to fill this in with eybrow pencil so that it did not
look as sparse as it was. He died my hair black and toyed
with the idea of shaving some of it, but we decided that a
shaved head rarely looks authentically bald, so instead of

subtracting hair from my own head I added hair to the photo of M. Mornay.

There was not very much else I could do. Good passport artists, with proper tools and years of experience, can perform extraordinary tricks. I know two such men, one in Athens and one in Manhattan, but I didn't know of anyone in Paris and had no time to find one. It would have been child's play for such an artist to alter Mornay's height and weight so that they corresponded to my own. As things stood, I had to rely on the fact that the average immigration officer is far too harried to spend too much time looking at a passport.

I left Paris late that afternoon. A different colon in the same Citroen drove me to the airport at Orly. I was wearing a medium-priced ready-made suit, and the cut of it showed me why Europeans have their clothes made to measure. Still, it fit my new role better than the applepicker's work clothes. I had them with me in a small imitation leather suitcase.

I flew to Geneva and Zurich. The following morning I went to the Bank Leu in Zurich where I have a signature-and-number account for money that can't conveniently accompany me into the States. I checked the balance and found that it stood at fifteen thousand Swiss francs, which is just under thirty-five hundred U.S. dollars.

I made them check it again, and they came up with the same figure. It was hard to believe that I had given so much money away in so short a time. There are a countless number of very good causes which I support, and it looked as though I had been supporting them even more munificently than I had realized.

"I thought there was more," I said.

"If Monsieur desires an accounting—"

"Oh, not at all," I said. "I trust you." That didn't sound right, and the manager looked very unhappy. "I mean I must have forgotten to carry," I said. "When I was subtracting. Something like that."

"But of course," he said, doubtfully.

"I'll have to get more to put in. As soon as I find

Phaedra and get back from—" I realized suddenly that I was running off at the mouth. "—from wherever I'm going," I finished.

I didn't want to close the account. I withdrew three thousand dollars in American funds, leaving so little that the bank obviously was only continuing to serve me out of a sense of noblesse oblige. I changed some of the dollars into Swiss francs and some into British pounds, and on a hunch I bought a couple hundred dollars' worth of gold from a wholesale jeweler on the Hirschengraben.

I killed time at a movie. I had already entered the theater before finding out that the film was one of those I had seen at Portsmouth, the Great Train Robbery thing, with all of the voices dubbed in German. The ending remained the same. Goddamned Scotland Yard caught the lot of them.

I took a taxi to the airport. I couldn't go home and I couldn't go back to England. I couldn't go to Kabul because the spies would tear me apart. I couldn't go to India or Pakistan because it would cost too much. I had only three thousand dollars and that would be barely enough to buy Phaedra's freedom. I couldn't go to Iran because the only direct flights went through either Athens or Istanbul, and I couldn't go to Athens or Istanbul for political reasons. I probably could have gone to Baghdad, but I wasn't sure how seriously the Iraqis took my involvement with the Kurdish rebels. I probably could have gone to Amman, unless the Jordanians knew me as a member of the Stern Gang.

I felt like Philip Nolan, the man without a country. I felt like a displaced person, a refugee, homeless, unwanted—

So where I went was Tel Aviv.

Chapter Seven

❀ ❀ ❀

Tourists entering Israel had their passports checked at length. Their luggage, too, received careful scrutiny. I had no way of knowing whether this was a matter of routine or if the inspectors had been tipped off to some special circumstances, but it was obvious in any event that M. Paul Mornay's Belgian passport would not get me into the Promised Land.

So Paul Mornay left the tourist line and joined another line composed of those planning to immigrate permanently to Israel, and in this line his passport did not receive a second glance. In Hebrew I told the attendant I was fulfilling my lifelong dream of returning to the homeland of my people. In Hebrew he told me that I would indeed be welcome. "You already speak the language," he said. "That will be of great value to you. And it encourages us to welcome newcomers from Europe. The country is drowning in a sea of Sephardim. And a sea of paper— consider the cursed forms we must fill out! But I shall gladly help you."

He gladly helped me, and in short order M. Paul Mornay had filed his preliminary applications for Israeli citizenship, stating that he was a Jew and had a Jewish mother, this last being Israel's *sine qua non* of Hebritude. "So you see that we are stricter than Hitler," the immigration officer joked. "With just one Jewish grandparent one could be admitted to Auschwitz, but one must have a Jewish mother to enter Israel."

I've no idea whether the real Paul Mornay, *aliveh sholem,* had a Jewish mother. Neither of my own parents were Jewish, although I do remember dimly that a sister of my father's had married a man named Moritz Stein-hardt, at which point the rest of the family ceased speaking with her. I have never been wholly certain whether she was ostracized because her husband was Jewish or German.

But as I filled out the immigration forms I felt a sudden bond of kinship with Minna's little friend Miguel. He stayed home on Jewish holidays, and I was a member of the Stern Gang and a citizen-to-be of Eretz Yisroel. As the rye bread advertisements put it, you don't *have* to be Jewish.

I stood at the window of Gershon's apartment and looked out at downtown Tel Aviv. "Many Americans compare our city to San Francisco," Gershon said, "but I have never been there. Do you notice the resemblance?"

I did now. In the taxi from the airport, I could think only that the driver punished his cab like a New Yorker.

"I have spoken to Zvi," Gershon went on. "You recall that he was with us in Prague when we first met you, Evan. He must stop at synagogue for his father's *yahrzeit* but will be over later. You remember also Ari and Haim?"

"Yes."

"Haim is with the Army in Sinai. It is months since I have seen him. And Ari. When you saw him, he still had both his legs. He lost one in the June war. His jeep took a direct hit, he was lucky to live at all. So now he has an administrative job in Hebron. A desk job, preparing orders for the management of the new lands of Greater Israel. It is no fun for him, as you can imagine. But there is talk of his running for a seat in the Knesset in the next elections. A wooden leg will produce almost as many votes in Israeli politics as a wooden head."

"In American politics, too."

"I have heard this." Gershon ran a hand through his thick black curls. "So much for old times. Zvi you will soon meet again, and the others must wait until your next visit. But you must be starving. I have an Arab girl who comes in twice a week to clean. She comes tomorrow, which accounts for the appearance of this apartment." He shrugged. "But I must do my own cooking, and my skills in that area limit me to sandwiches. Are you a very close observer of the dietary laws, Evan?"

"Not really."

"A bit of butter on a meat sandwich—"

"Would not bother me at all." ·

"Thank God," Gershon said. He returned from the kitchen with a plate of sandwiches on thinly-sliced dark rye. I took a bite and looked at him.

"Zebra sandwiches, Evan. You have probably not had anything of the sort in America."

"Never."

"The flesh of the zebra is virtually unknown outside of Israel. It is said that zebra tastes remarkably like the flesh of the prohibited swine, yet the zebra parteth the hoof in obedience to the Mosaic injunction. These sandwiches, for example, may taste rather like ham sandwiches."

"There is a remarkable resemblance."

"The zebra is a heaven-sent animal." Gershon's eyes shone. "For example, a portion of his flesh when fried is an exceptionally good accompaniment to eggs for breakfast. They say that it tastes much like bacon, but of course I have no basis for comparison."

I finished one of the sandwiches. "The, uh, zebras," I said. "Are they imported?"

"Oh, no. The raising of zebras is a native Israeli industry. Yet perhaps because the breeders wish to protect their secrets, one rarely actually sees these fine black-and-white striped animals anywhere in the nation. However on a drive through the countryside one might hear their characteristic cry from within one of their pens."

"What sound do zebras make?"

"Oink," Gershon said. "Ah, Evan, my comrade, one requires a Talmudic turn of mind to contend with life in modern Israel. Between the theocracy and the round-shouldered ghetto dwellers and the lice-ridden Sephardim, one has one's hands full in letting the country take her place among the nations of the world. Do you know that there are fools who would return Sinai to Nasser and the Golan Heights to Syria? There are even those who would give back Jerusalem to Hussein. But not a square foot of territory shall be returned."

"There is talk that Sinai and the west bank of the Jordan might be given back as part of a peace settlement," I said.

"Peace?" Gershon sighed heavily. "Peace," he said. "Peace is a bottle of beer, Evan." This statement confused me until a while later, after Zvi had joined us, Gershon served us some local beer. The brand name was Shalom. "We have no need of peace, Evan. In what sort of war does the victor make concessions to the vanquished? Almost a year-and-a-half ago, in June, after years of provocation, the Arab attack was crushed in a lightning war of six days. Now the deserts shall bloom and we shall have renewed living space for the Jews of the world who will return to their homeland. Who can even speak of peace? Every day there are new border incidents. The people grow strong with victory. They have a sense of their historic mission. . . ."

The mind plays tricks, translating phrases from one language to another. Lightning war becomes *blitzkrieg,* living space metamorphoses into *lebensraum.* I remembered the Sternist oath I had sworn in a cold-water flat on Attorney Street, pledging to work for the restoration of Israel to its historic boundaries from Dan to Beersheba on both sides of the Jordan. The language of the oath, I realized, was somewhat inconclusive; Dan and Beersheba set the north-south limits, but just how far "Greater Israel" might extend east and west of the Jordan was subject to varying interpretation.

Unwelcome thoughts. I bit deeply into my zebra sandwich, chewed, swallowed. And, when Gershon paused, I began to talk about Afghanistan and a girl named Deborah Horowitz.

I went over the story a second time when Zvi joined us. The tale of Phaedra's fate could not have had a more appreciative audience. A nice Jewish girl kidnaped by Arabs. I explained that the Afghans were not Arabs. But they were Moslems, were they not? I admitted that they were. Moslems, Arabs, it was the same thing, was it not? Well, I said, one could stretch a point. Zvi cited the commandment in the Torah that the Daughters of Israel should not prostitute themselves. This sidetracked Gershon momentarily; he began reminiscing about a Yemenite immigrant in Jaffa, a hooker with almost unbelievable muscular control. Zvi glanced sharply at him and he abandoned the subject in midsentence.

"We will go with you," Zvi said, firmly. "We will rescue this Deborah and return her to the land of her forefathers. We shall lead her out of the land of Afghanistan, out of the house of bondage."

The thought was a tempting one. I extended the metaphor mentally and imagined the waters parting so that Zvi and Gershon and Phaedra and I might cross the Arabian Sea on dry land.

"You have work here," I said. "And the rescue of Deborah may be accomplished with little difficulty." I wished I believed this. "I need only to get from here to Jordan. Then I will be able to proceed by myself."

"Ah. You wish to enter Jordan?"

"Yes."

"But this will be no problem for you, will it, Evan?" Zvi smiled. "You are an American and can enter Jordan at will."

Gershon said, "But he has been to Israel. Will Hussein admit him?"

"Perhaps. The Egyptians are stricter about that sort of thing, of course, but the Jordanians—"

I cut in, explaining that I didn't happen to have an American passport handy, and couldn't enter Jordan with it if I did. I would have to slip across the border. "I suppose this would have been easier before the war," I added, "when the Jordanians held the west bank. But if you could tell me the best place to cross—"

The two exchanged glances. Zvi said something to Gershon about the absolute secrecy of their mission, and Gershon pointed out that I was a loyal Sternist and had performed great service in Czechoslovakia, not to mention my generous financial gifts to the organization. Zvi thought this over and decided in my favor.

"We will be part of a group crossing the border tonight," he said. "It is possible that you could join us."

"I am grateful."

"It will be necessary for you to dress as an Arab. We can provide suitable clothing, but it would be advantageous if you could learn a few words of Arabic in the hours that remain."

I said in Arabic that this would present little difficulty. Zvi raised an eyebrow. "Next you will tell us that you can ride a camel."

"I will tell you no such thing."

"Ah. But you will learn. We drive east to Rammun. Do you know it? It is not far from Jericho, but Joshua did not level its walls and so it is less well known. A small old town, most of it abandoned when the Jordanians withdrew across the river. Our camels are waiting there."

Chapter Eight

❀ ❀ ❀

In the seventeenth century an Afghan nobleman named Ali Mardan Khan demonstrated his public spirit by raising national monuments of one sort or another in and around Kabul. The greatest of these was an arcaded and roofed bazaar called Chihâr Châtâ. Its four arms had an aggregate length of about 600 feet, with a breadth of about thirty. Kabul is a beautifully situated city to begin with, nestled among the mountains with peaks rising on three sides of the city. It is a city of striking architecture, and Chihâr Châtâ, it would seem, was something rather extraordinary.

In 1842 a British general named Pollock evacuated Kabul. On the way out he leveled Chihâr Châtâ to punish the city for its treachery. Leveled it. Knocked the whole thing down, that is, so that all the king's horses and all the king's men couldn't.

I couldn't really blame General Pollock. Kabul was that kind of a town. Treacherous.

By the time I had been in the city for all of twenty-one hours, they had made three attempts on my life.

That's treacherous.

But wait a minute—wasn't he in Israel a minute ago? Something about getting on a camel?

True. Except that it wasn't a minute ago, really, but

91

several weeks ago, and since that camel (and if you have never ridden a camel you cannot possibly know how bad they are) there had been donkeys and mules and broken down cars and a truck and a lot of walking and, all in all, an almost incredible spate of boredom. Well, not boredom, exactly. It wasn't boring sitting around a mountain campfire with a band of Kurdish rebels. It wasn't boring at a village a few miles from Teheran, eating sheep's bladder stuffed with cracked wheat and almonds and apricots, which is at least a thousand times better than it sounds. The mountain views through Afghan Turkistan were never boring, nor were the languages (some new, some half-known) or the people.

It was just such a grind. I kept on the move constantly and I just couldn't find any real way to speed things up. The distances were great, the roads fairly primitive, and my own lack of valid papers kept me away from main roads and speedier methods of transportation.

So it took a while. It took more time to live through than it does to put down a quick summary of what happened. What happened was that virtually nothing happened, and I stayed alive and wound up in Kabul, and all of a sudden the rest of the world decided I had lived too long and to too little purpose and did what it could to change all that.

I reached the outskirts of Kabul after nightfall, and it was another hour by the time I got as far as the center of town. I stopped at a coffee house, where an old man with a wispy beard and stainless steel teeth was playing an instrument that was a cross between an oud and a round-backed mandolin. I had a cup of coffee—very thick, very bitter—and a pilaf of cracked wheat and currants. I kibitzed a backgammon game, had another cup of coffee, and asked a fellow kibitzer if he knew a man named Amanullah.

"I know Amanullah the Seller of Fish, and Amanullah the Son of Hadi of the Book Stall."

"Perhaps he means Amanullah of the Lamps and Old Artifacts," one of the players suggested.

"Or Amanullah Who Has But One Eye. Is this the Amanullah you seek, *kâzzih?*"

Amanullah, it seemed, was as rare in Afghanistan as flies in a latrine. Kabul was positively buzzing with Amanullahs. I explained rather haltingly, which is the only way I've ever learned to speak Pushtu (also known as Pakhsto and Pakkhto and Pashto). It is the language of the Afghans, and it is one of those unnecessarily complex Asian tongues to which I attribute the illiteracy of such a large portion of the population. Of course they can't read and write. There are thirty-seven classes of verbs, thirteen intransitive and twenty-four transitive. No one should have to contend with that sort of nonsense.

Well. What I explained haltingly was that I had traveled upon a journey of many miles in search of a man named Amanullah whom I had never met and whose likeness I had never seen.

"I know not the name of his father," I said. "Amanullah is a large man with white hair, long white hair. He is a seller of slaves."

"Ah," said the kibitzer, thoughtfully. "Amanullah of the White Hair."

"Amanullah of the Selling of the Slaves," said the backgammon player.

"Do you know where I may find him?"

"I know of no such man," said the kibitzer.

"He is unknown to me," said the other one.

I had always wondered where the old vaudeville acts went when the Orpheum circuit dried up. I went back to my own table and had another cup of coffee. Then I left a few copper coins on the table and went outside, and as I was slipping my little change purse back into the folds of this robelike Afghan garment I was wearing, it fell to the ground. The change purse, not the garment.

So I bent down to get it, and my turban blew off.

That seemed silly. There was hardly any wind at all, surely not enough wind to blow a turban off somebody's head. I said, "What the hell?" which probably means nothing at all in Pushtu, and I turned around and picked up the turban, and there was a dagger sticking in it.

If I hadn't dropped the change purse, the dagger would have landed in the small of my back or thereabouts.

I looked around and didn't see anyone. I looked at the dagger again to make sure it was still there, and it was. I was suddenly reminded of all those terrible movie bits where a guy walks into a bar in Boston and asks questions about a man named Kyriatos, then gets on a jet to St. Louis and charters a private plane to the Sun Valley slopes. Halfway up the ski lift somebody sticks an automatic in his back and a voice says, "I am Kyriatos. What do you want with me?"

I'd always objected to that sort of garbage in the movies. But here I had gone into a coffeehouse and asked some dumb questions about Amanullah, whom evidently no one had ever heard of and cared not at all about, and then I took three steps out the door and somebody put a dagger in my turban.

It couldn't be connected, I decided. That was the trouble with secret agentry as a career. It fostered paranoia. After a few years in the field you couldn't get mugged by a junkie without reading international intrigue into the affair. Every penny-ante burglar who knocked over your apartment took on the trappings of a spy searching for mysterious documents. Obviously some Afghan lowlife had tried to do me in for the purse I had just dropped. Or, if you prefer, some ardent nationalist had tried to do to me what he had just heard me doing to his language. But none of this, obviously, had anything whatsoever to do with Phaedra Harrow or Amanullah of the White Hair.

I removed the dagger from my turban and found a place for it in my robe. It was a very impressive affair, that dagger. The handle was some sort of bone with an elaborate inlay of mother-of-pearl. The blade was of fine steel with a geometrical pattern etched on either side. It was the sort of weapon that used to be found in English gentlemen in very early Agatha Christie novels.

The idea of resuming my search for Amanullah made

me a little nervous at first. But I told myself I was being silly, and after telling myself this for a few minutes I began to believe it, and off I went on the trail of Amanullah of the White Hair.

The next few hours produced a few offers of slaves for sale and very little else. Slavery, I learned, is illegal in Afghanistan, just as off-track betting on horse races is illegal in the United States. From what I could see, it was about as hard to purchase a slave in Kabul as it was to get a bet down in Manhattan. Perhaps it was even easier, because the slave-selling business seemed more competitive than bookmaking. I kept shuffling around asking for Amanullah the Slave Trader, and I kept finding myself referred to other men with slaves for sale who did not, sad to say, happen to be Amanullah.

Kabul gets very quiet between midnight and dawn. Almost everything closes and the streets are empty. There was a cold dry wind blowing down from the north, and I spent the early hours of the morning huddled in the doorway of a saddler's shop, trying to get warm and organize my thoughts. The one was as hard as the other.

The sun came up in a hurry. I shook the dust out of my robes and resumed wandering through Kabul, asking more questions, nibbling dough cakes here, sipping coffee there, and gradually finding my way to the oldest section of the city. The streets were extremely narrow, with the huts on either side taking up where the street left off. Motor vehicles could not negotiate those streets. Heavy-boned Afghan work horses and little Persian donkeys plodded patiently through the streets. The air was heavy with an air pollution centuries older than carbon monoxide. The sun rose higher in the sky, and the heat, trapped by the too-close huts and shacks, became oppressive.

And in the early afternoon a sidewalk vendor of doubtful sausages closed his good eye a moment in thought, stroked his beard with tobacco-stained fingers, opened his eye again, and nodded pensively at me. "A great man with white hair that hangs to his shoulders," he said. "A man with a furious appetite, a man who eats day and night and

whose belly would press through his robes if it could. A
man who deals with the foreigners, with the men of Europe and India and with the sons of Han from the Chinese
hills, purchasing women from them and placing them in
houses in the countryside where the miners use them as
maradóosh. Is this the Amanullah you seek, *kâzzih?"*

"It is, old one."

"He is the brother of the husband of the sister of my
wife."

"Ah."

"You have business with him, *kâzzih*? You have wom-
en to sell?"

"I have business with Amanullah."

"By your accent you have come on a journey of many
miles. You are an Afghan?"

"My mother was an Afghan."

"Ah. If you go to the Café of the Four Sisters, *kâzzih,* you find him there. Amanullah. You tell him you
bear good wishes of Tarsheen of the Sausage Pot. May
your business prosper, *kâzzih."*

"May your road run downhill and the wind be at your
back, Tarsheen."

"Blessings attend you, *kâzzih."*

The Café of the Four Sisters was a little wineshop
deep in the heart of the old part of town. Two of the
sisters passed among customers seated on cut-down wine
barrels. One brought me a glass of sweet white wine. If all
Afghan women looked like the two sisters, I could understand why Amanullah's business was prosperous. I
couldn't remember ever seeing a more unspeakably ugly
woman.

Unspeakable or not, I spoke to her. I asked for Amanullah and was pleased to note that she knew precisely
whom I meant. We didn't even go through the vaudeville
routine aimed at defining precisely which Amanullah I
had in mind.

"He comes here every day, *kâzzih."*

"Is he here now, then?" I had seen no one who fit the description.

"Ah, but he is gone."

"He returns soon?" There is, incidentally, no future tense in Pushtu, which is why the conversations reported up to now have been somewhat stilted. Just a present tense and an imperfect tense. The present is used to convey present time and all future and conditional time. The imperfect covers all past time. "He comes again to the café this afternoon?"

"It is said that he goes on business to the west. He returns by nightfall, but if he stops here for wine I know not."

"I thank you, sister."

I set my wine glass down. Someone brushed my table and nearly knocked it over. I rescued the glass, raised it, set it down untasted. Something struck a chord in my mind but I couldn't pick out the notes. That man who had passed my table—

I got up, glanced around for him. He was just leaving the cafe. I followed him out, lost him in the crowd. I caught a glimpse of his small eyes and spade-shaped black beard and then he was gone.

I returned to the cafe. In the corner an old man was coughing violently, pounding the earthen floor with his fists. His face had a bluish cast to it and he seemed to be dying of something. A few of his friends were clustered around him. The rest of the drinkers ignored him.

I got back to my table, but my wine glass was gone. I decided that the waitress must have picked it up, and I remembered how cloyingly sweet the wine had been and decided I didn't want any more anyway.

On the way out the door I heard the death rattle in the old man's throat.

The third time was the charm.

I don't really think anyone would have figured it out on the basis of a simple dagger through the turban. I suppose, though, that I should have gotten the message in the

Café of the Four Sisters. My own wine glass gone, an old wino coughing himself to death, a man who looked familiar passing my table and almost spilling my wine—I guess anyone with half a brain would have figured out that the man with the spade-shaped beard had put some poison in my glass, which the other man had cadged when I ducked out of the café. If I had read it all somewhere I'm sure I would have figured it out for myself, but instead I was living through it, and it's always harder that way.

If nothing else, I was certain that I didn't know anybody in Afghanistan. I know people almost everywhere, and on the whole I found it quite remarkable that I didn't know anybody in Afghanistan, since a friend in need in Kabul would have been a friend indeed, indeed. And if no one knew me, there would be no reason for anyone to be putting daggers in my turban or poison in my wine.

I went back to the Café of the Four Sisters a couple of times in the course of the afternoon. Amanullah never did get there. I spent the rest of my time sort of wandering around and getting the feel of the city. It was what guidebooks call a study in contrasts, with broad avenues as wide as the streets of the old quarter were narrow. There were a few foreigners in the city, most of them Pakistanis from Kashmir, a few Russian types of one sort or another. Mostly, though, there were Afghans, and most of them were dressed more or less as I was—leather sandals, a loose fitting robe more like an ancient Roman toga than anything else, and a sort of turban.

By sunset I was hungry. I had started drifting back in the general direction of the Four Sisters, and I stopped along the way at a hut from the central chimney of which wafted the odor of broiling mutton. I went inside and stood at a long counter. A thickset man took a mutton steak off the charcoal fire, sprinkled a mixture of unidentifiable spices over it, and slapped it onto a cast iron plate, which he placed on the counter before me. There were no knives or forks. When in Rome, I thought, and picked the meat up in my hands and began gnawing at it. Out of the corner of my eye I noticed another man glaring at me. I turned. All of the other diners, I saw, had selected knives and forks from a bin against the far wall. All of the other diners looked at me as if I were a barbarian. Chastened, I went to the bin for knife and fork, returned, and went to work on the food.

While I was eating, the chef spooned a mixture of cracked wheat and rice onto my plate. The mutton was rare on the inside and black on the outside and very tangy. The cracked wheat and rice was a successful combination. I noticed another man drinking some sort of beerish concoction, and when the chef passed my way again I pointed at my fellow diner and made drinking motions. It turned out to be beer, but with an unusual taste to it that I finally identified as cashew nuts. This didn't seem to make sense, as the cashew nut is native to the Western Hemisphere, and world trade would have to advance to an extraordinary degree before South Americans took to shipping cashew nuts to Afghanistan breweries. I found out subsequently that an Afghan nut vaguely similar to the cashew is used to flavor the beer.

I had two liters of the beer and finished my mutton steak. I ordered another beer—it wasn't the best beer I'd ever tasted, but there was something habit-forming about the taste—and I drank a little of this, and then I realized that I would have to get rid of some old beer in order to make room for the rest of the new beer.

There was no lavatory as such, just a trough at the base of the back wall. I went out there and did the sort of thing one does at urinals, and as I was concluding this operation the little hut blew up.

For an insane moment I thought I had done it. The Man Who Pees Dynamite. I suppose that's the feeling a woodpecker gets if he goes to work on a tree just as the lumberman gives it the final chop. After all, it was a pretty extraordinary experience. One minute I was urinating on this building, and the next minute the goddamned building was gone.

The damage was close to total, the destruction approached utter, and the chaos was absolute. There was the sound of the explosion followed by complete silence. This held for maybe ten seconds. Then everybody in Kabul set up a hue and cry.

The blast knocked me flat on my back, which was probably just as well, because most of what was inside the little restaurant was blown outside, and it wouldn't have been wise to be standing in the way. By the time I was back on my feet, neither bloody nor unbowed, the chaos had reached absolute pitch. There were sirens wailing in the distance, and it occurred to me that I was in what might well turn out to be a bad place for a foreigner without papers.

So I manfully ignored the cries of help rising from the near-dead, and heroically resisted the temptation to come to the aid of my fellow man, and didn't even go back to look for my beer. I don't think I'd have had much luck anyway; the counter was gone, and the charcoal stove, and the chairs, and most of the people. I got the hell out of there as fast as my legs could carry me, which turned out to be somewhat faster than I had suspected. I raced down the block and around the corner, and I very nearly collided with the man with the spade-shaped black beard.

He stared at me. "You're alive!"

"You speak English," I said, cleverly.

"Curse you, Tanner! What does it take to kill you?"

He pulled out the world's biggest pistol and stuck it in my face. "This time you don't get away," he said. "Knives don't work on you, bombs don't work on you, it's impossible to drown you. But with a hole in your damned head perhaps it will be different."

"Wait a minute," I said, reasonably. "Do you realize what you're doing? Do you have any idea?"

He stared at me.

"You're making a terrible mistake."

"Talk," he demanded.

"Well," I said, and kicked him in the groin.

Chapter Nine

❀ ❀ ❀

Nothing succeeds like a kick in the groin.

I suppose it must be at least partly psychological. Even when the kick is wide of the mark, men tend to double up and moan for a few moments before they realize that nothing hurts. The mere suggestion of a kick in the cubes is harrowing, and I gave my bearded friend more than the suggestion. I got him right on target, and I put enough into the kick so that it was unlikely that he would ever sire children. Which, considering the type of genes he'd be likely to pass on and the already crowded state of the world, was just as well.

He fell apart. He dropped the gun, which I picked up and tucked into my robe along with the dagger that was my souvenir of his first visit. He dropped himself, too, sprawling on the ground, clutching his crotch with both hands and making perfectly horrible sounds.

Everyone ignored us.

I'm damned if I know why. Whether it was simply that the bombed-out restaurant was a greater source of interest than an argument between two strangers, or whether the basic sense of privacy of the Afghan led him to choose not to get involved I cannot say, but whatever the cause we were left quite alone. I got my bearded friend to his feet and walked him around the corner and into an alleyway. I doubled his arm up behind him so that we would walk where I wanted to walk. He wasn't very good at walking, choosing to stagger with his thighs as far apart as he could contrive, but I got him into the alley and propped him against the wall, and he stayed propped for almost five seconds before crumpling into a heap on the ground.

"If you're going to shoot someone," I said, reasonably, "you should just go ahead and do it. It serves no point to tell him about it first. It just gives him a chance to try and do something about it."

"You kicked me," he said.

"Good thinking. I'm glad you're in condition to think, because this is important. I want you clowns to stop trying to kill me."

He set his jaw and glared at me.

"Because there's really no point to it. You know, I had forgotten all about you morons." I switched to Russian, remembering that they had been speaking it on the boat. "You and Yaakov and Daly and the rest of you. I forgot all about you. You wouldn't believe what I went through getting here. Did you ever ride a camel? Or try to convince a Kurd that you aren't spying for the Baghdad government? Or eat zebra sandwiches in Tel Aviv? Of course I forgot about you. It was a pleasure to forget about you."

"We thought you died in the water."

"Not quite."

"And then Peder saw you last night. He saw you enter the town, and Raffo followed you and tried to kill you as you left the coffee house." He lowered his eyes. "He said it was as if you were guided by demons. You dropped to the ground even as the knife was in the middle of the air."

"Well, the demons told me to."

"Now I have tried twice and failed twice." He looked up at me. "You will kill me now?"

"No."

"You will not kill me?"

"I'd like nothing better," I said, "but it would be a waste of time. If I kill you they'll just put somebody else on the job. Look, I want you to take them a message. You seem to think that I'm a threat to you—"

"You know our plans."

"Not really."

"And you have come to Afghanistan to thwart them."

"No, definitely not. Why would I want to do a thing like that?"

"You are a spy and an assassin."

"Be that as it may, I couldn't care less about you and your plans. And I don't really know what they are, except that you're going to overthrow the government of Afghanistan—"

"Ha! You know!"

"Well, I didn't think you were over here to get a concession to breed Afghan hounds. But I don't know the date or the reason or—"

"You arrive in Kabul on the 14th of November and try to have us believe you do not know the coup is to be on the 25th?"

"The 25th?"

"Ha! You know!"

"Well, you just told me, you cretin." I turned, glanced at the mouth of the alleyway. We were still quite alone. "Look at it this way," I said. "If I knew anything, or if I cared at all, I could inform someone. That might make sense. But since you already had a make on me, why would I come into Kabul myself? Why wouldn't I have my organization send someone you don't know about?"

"It is said that you are very shrewd."

I looked at the heavens. The sky had grown dark, and I didn't blame it a bit. He said, "If you would not sabotage our plot, why are you here in Kabul?"

"I'm looking for a girl."

"You'll have to go to a whorehouse. The ordinary girls, they will not even talk to strangers."

"You don't understand. I'm looking for a girl I happen to know. She was kidnaped and taken to Afghanistan."

"And where is she?"

"In a whorehouse."

"Ha! You *will* have to go to a whorehouse!" His face lighted up, then clouded over. "You talk in riddles," he said. "You speak nonsense, you are impossible to understand. You tell me there is something you must say to me, and then you kick me in my poor testicles. You told us on the boat you could not speak Russian, and now at this very moment you and I are speaking Russian fluently."

"Well, your accent's not so hot."

"I am Bulgarian."

"Make things easy for yourself," I said in Bulgarian. "Just so you get the message. Speak to me in Bulgarian as well, and we shall be at ease with one another, and you can go back to Yaakov with the message, and—"

"You know of Yaakov."

"Well, I met the sonofabitch. Of course I know of him."

"It is all a trick," he said mournfully. "You said on the boat that a man was overboard, and this was not so, and when we looked you were suddenly overboard. Now you say that you will not kill me, so of course I know that you will."

"I'd like to."

"Ha!"

"More and more I'd like to." I thought of the restaurant where I'd had that fine mutton steak, that cashew-flavored beer. The restaurant and all the hungry people in it were now a thing of the past, all because of this little bastard with his bomb.

"But killing you does me more harm than good," I said. "Look, let's try it on one more time. I'm not interested in you. I don't give a damn about your plot or the government of Afghanistan or anything else except the girl I came to Afghanistan to find. I'm not even sure I give a damn about her either, but I certainly care more about her than any of the rest of you. And I also care about staying alive. I don't want knives in my turban or poison in my wine or walls that explode when I take a leak on them. Don't interrupt me. All I want is to be left alone.

I'll let you go, and you'll go back and tell them that. Right?"

"You will not kill me?"

"Good thinking."

His eyes grew crafty. "You are with the Central Intelligence Agency, perhaps?"

"So that's what was grabbing you."

"Who is grabbing me?"

"No, forget it. No, I'm not with the Central Intelligence Agency. As a matter of fact, the Central Intelligence Agency and I don't get along very well."

"You are an enemy of the CIA?"

"Well, I suppose you could put it that way, if you don't mind stretching a point. You could even say I'm a great friend of Russia if you want. A supporter of the Soviet Union. An ally of the People's Republic of Bulgaria, if it makes you happy."

"Ha! The Soviet Union!"

"Sure."

"Ha! Bulgaria!"

"Ha! indeed," I said. "So you'll tell your boss, okay? Yaakov, the one with all the knees and elbows and teeth. Tell him I'm a good guy and I just came here to get my glasses cleaned. And tell him to for God's sake stop sending people to kill me. I don't like it."

He nodded.

"And now," I said, "I am not doing this because I hate you, but simply because I don't trust you. I know it's mean of me to think it, but I've got a feeling that you might try to follow me."

"I would never do this," he said.

"Somehow you fail to convince me. I even have a hunch that, given insufficient time for reflection, you might have another try at killing me."

"I am not such a man."

I aimed a kick at his groin. I checked it, but the mere thought of it was enough to make him double up, hands at crotch. It was no great trick to grab his head and rap it a couple of times against the wall. Not too hard, because I

wanted my message delivered to Yaakov. Not too soft,
either, because I wasn't that crazy about my little bearded
friend. If he had a headache when he woke up, that was
fine with me.

I slipped out of the mouth of the alleyway. I didn't just
walk out, the way I would have done earlier. I found my
way to the end of the alley and stuck my head out very
carefully and looked to the left and to the right, and then
I scurried out and disappeared into the shadows on the
other side of the street.

If all of these fools didn't know any better than to waste
time killing me, at least I could be on my guard. There
was no point in making their work easy for them.

A man named Arthur Hook had described him as a
great hulking wog with white hair to his shoulders. A man
named Tarsheen of the Sausage Pot added that he had a
furious appetite and a belly that would press through his
robes if it could. They were both right. Amanullah the son
of Ba'aloth the son of Pezran the son of D'hon was all this
and more.

He sort of hung. His hair hung straight to his shoulders, white as a Southern jury and limp as a eunuch. His
body was appallingly fat all over, and the fat drooped.
Someone must have slammed the door while his head was
in the oven, because his face had fallen all over the place.
His eyes were huge and very blue, contrasting nicely with
his brown teeth. His ears were positively gigantic, with
huge lobes, and if he could have contrived to flap them he
could have flown away like Dumbo the Flying Elephant,
whom he probably outweighed. While I introduced myself
he engulfed a salad, a large wedge of cheese, two liters of
beer and a chunk of bread the size of a small loaf. He
didn't even seem to be eating. He seemed to inhale his
food, to breathe it into his belly.

And he was, all of this notwithstanding, an exceedingly
charming man. Good will was an aura around him. I sat
down across the table from him fully prepared to despise

him, and from the onset I found it impossible to do other
than like him.

"So you bring greetings from Tarsheen, eh?" He belched
rather delicately. "Tarsheen of the Sausage Pot. He is,
let me see—"

"The husband of the sister of the wife of your brother."

"Why, *kâzzih*, you understand my family ties better
than I do myself! It is as you say. You tasted the sausages
of Tarsheen? None better are sold in the streets of Kabul.
In this wineshop, though, one may obtain the best food
anywhere in the city."

"I thought there was only wine."

"For me there is food. For others, no. I eat here constantly, it is my pleasure in life." He erupted with laughter. "As if I must tell you this, eh?" He slapped his
abdomen. "As if my belly does not testify amply to my
source of happiness?" He slapped it again. "But I eat and
offer nothing, it is not seemly. You wish nourishment?"

"I ate not an hour ago."

"An hour after eating I am famished. You wish wine?"

"Perhaps beer."

He ordered it, and another of the ugly sisters brought
it. Somewhere along the line I asked him why it tasted of
cashews, and he explained about the nut with which they
flavored it. When I finished the beer he ordered me another.

"Now, *kâzzih*," he said eventually, "I suspect you
wish to discuss business. Is it not so?"

"It is so."

"And your business is what?"

"A woman."

"Only one woman? I see. You buy or you sell?"

"I buy."

"You have preference as to type? Young or old, tall or
short, Eastern or Western? Fat? Slender? Dark or light?
Or would you examine my poor stock and determine what
strikes your fancy?"

"I want a girl named Phaedra," I said.

"A name?" He shrugged massively. "But of what importance is a name? To be honest, I never bother learning the names of the girls I handle. But if you wish a girl with such a name—how is it called?"

"Phaedra."

"A most unusual name in this part of the world. Is it Hindu?"

"It's Greek."

"How extraordinary! The name, though, what does it matter? You select a girl, you pay her price, she is yours to do with as you wish. If you wish to call her Phaedra, so she is called. If you wish to call her Dunghill, to Dunghill does she answer. Is it not so, *kâzzih*?"

I sighed. I wasn't quite getting my point across. I took it from the top again and explained that I was looking for a girl whom he had already handled, a girl he had already purchased as a slave.

"A girl brought here to me?"

"Yes."

"Ah, that is another matter entirely. When did this occur?"

I told him.

"So many months? A problem." He picked up a roll, broke it in half, sopped up salad oil with it, and gobbled it up. "I bought and sold many girls that month, *kâzzih*. How would I know one from another?"

I told him the seller was an Englishman and that the girl was part of a shipment of half a dozen English girls. I dragged out my picture of Phaedra and gave him a look at it. He studied it for a long time.

"I remember the girl," he said.

"Thank God."

"She is Greek? I did not think—"

"She is American."

"American, but her name is Greek. The world has more questions than answers, is it not so? I remember the girl, the others that she came with. The demand was strong at that time. All of those girls were placed almost immediately. You would do well to forget her, *kâzzih*."

I stared. "Why?"

"It is sad." He rolled his huge blue eyes. *"Kâzzih,* if you loved her, you should have purchased her freedom before ever she came to Afghanistan. A man falls in love with a slave girl, and he does not think she is ever taken from him. He does not anticipate this. And then she is sold, and sold again, and only then does he regret waiting so long. And by that time it is too late."

"Why is it too late?"

"Ah, *kâzzih,* drink your beer. These are sad times."

"Is she alive?"

"Do I know? When I have sold a woman my interest in her ceases. She is no longer my property. It would be immoral for me to maintain concern in her. She lives, she dies, I do not know. Nor does it matter."

"But if she is alive I will purchase her freedom—"

"I knew you would say this, *kâzzih.* You are young, eh? You have few years and no white hairs. The young speak too quickly. There is a proverb in my country, a saying of the ancients, that the old lizard sleeps in the sun and the young lizard chases his tail. Do you understand?"

"Not really."

"Ah, the sorrow of it! But this slave girl, this Phaedra. She has been two months in one of the houses, she has served for two months as *maradóon.* Do you not know what two months as maradóon does to a girl? You can use her no longer, my young friend. Let her remain with the rest of the maradóosh. Whatever you paid for her would be too much."

"But that's horrible!"

"The life of a slave is horrible. It is true. The whole system of humans owning humans, you might call me a firebrand to say, so, *kâzzih,* but the entire institution of slavery should be brought to an end."

"And yet you deal in slaves."

"A man must eat," he said, decimating the cheese. "A man must eat. If there are to be slaves bought and sold, it is as well that I profit by their purchase and sale as another."

"But," I said, and stopped. America is too full of

socialists who work on Wall Street and humanitarians who
sell guns; I had met Amanullah in sufficient other guises as
to know the foolishness of arguing with him on this point.

"But," I said, starting over, "you said that I neglected
to purchase Phaedra when I might have done so."

"Yes."

"Before coming here, she was not a slave."

"But this cannot be. The man who brought her, she was
his slave."

"No."

"But of course she was!" He lifted his mug and was less
than thrilled to find it empty. He roared for beer, and the
ugly sister came running with full mugs for both of us.

"Of course she was a slave," he repeated. "All of those
girls, all the girls I buy are slaves. If they were not slaves,
how could they be sold?"

"You do not know?"

"Kâzzih, what are you talking about?"

"Oh," I said. "Oh, I see. I'll be damned. You didn't
know."

"Kâzzih!"

So I went over it for him, the whole thing. I told him
how Arthur Hook had worked his little gambit in London, conning a covey of quail into thinking they were
taking the Grand Tour and then selling them before they
knew what was happening.

Amanullah was horrified.

"But that cannot be," he said. "One does not become
maradóon in such a manner."

"These girls did."

"One cannot be sold into slavery for no good reason.
Not even in my grandfather's time did such barbarism
occur. It is unthinkable. There is an Afghan proverb,
perhaps you know it. 'The lamb finds its mother in tall
grass.' Is it not so?"

"No question about it."

"Unthinkable. A girl is sold into slavery by her parents,
as with the girls of China and Japan. Or she is captured as
booty in tribal warfare. Or she is the daughter of a slave

and thus enslaved from birth. Or she chooses slavery as an alternative to death or imprisonment for her crimes. Or she is given in slavery by her husband when she proves barren, although I must say that this barbarism occurs only among several tribes to the west of us and I could no more strongly condemn it. But these methods which I mention, they are the ways in which a slave is brought to me, these are the elements of her background. 'Neither sow in autumn nor harvest in the spring,' it is a saying of ours, a saying of great antiquity. That someone should sell me a girl who was not already enslaved—and he has done this before, you say? This Englishman?"

"Yes."

"He offends me and wrongs me. He makes me party to his evil. You must draw his likeness for me, and when he returns to Kabul I shall have him put to death."

"That would be impossible."

"I am not without influence in high places."

"You'd really need it," I said. "He's already dead."

"He was executed by his government?"

"He was executed by me."

The eyes widened, the jaw dropped. Astonishment registered on Amanullah's pendulous face. Radiance slowly replaced it and the fat Afghan slave trader beamed at me.

"You have done me a great favor," he said. "The man did me a great wrong. Ah, you might say, but he did not cheat me! And this is true. I made a fine profit on every girl purchased from him. But he made me a partner in his sinfulness. He made me a criminal, a corrupt one. May the flames torture him throughout eternity, may the worms that eat his flesh grow sick from the taste of him, may his image fade from human memory, may it be as if he had never been."

"Amen."

"More beer!"

After more beer, after an infinity of more beer, after a veritable tidal wave of more beer, Amanullah and I had repaired to his house, a brick and stone edifice on the northeast outskirts of the city. There he made me a small pot of coffee and poured himself—guess what?—another beer.

"But coffee for you, *kâzzih*. You have no head for beer, eh? It makes you sleepy and stupid."

Sleepy, no. Stupid? Perhaps.

"You like my city, *kâzzih*? You enjoy Kabul?"

"It's very pleasant."

"A peaceful city. A city of great wealth and beauty, although there are yet the poor with us. Great beauty. The mountains, sheltering Kabul from the winds and rain. The freshness of the air, the purity of the waters."

The only problem, I thought, was that a person could get killed around here.

"And in recent years there is so much development, so many roads being constructed, so much progress being made. For years we Afghans wished only to be left to ourselves. We asked nothing else. Merely that the British leave us alone. And the others who dominated us, but largely the British. And so at last the British were gone, and we lived under our own power, and it was good.

"But now the Russians give us money to build a road, and so we take the money and dig up a perfectly good road and replace it with a new one built with the Russian money. And the Americans come to us and say, 'You took aid from the Russians, now you must take aid from us or we will be insulted and offended.' Who would offend such a powerful nation? And so we permit the Americans to come into our country and construct a hydroelectric power station. And the Russians see the hydroelectric power station and force upon us a canning factory. The Americans retaliate by shipping bad-smelling chemicals to be plowed into the soils of our farms. And so it goes. So it goes."

He hoisted his beer, drank deeply. "But I talk to excess. I am a man of excess. I feel that anything worth doing is worth doing to excess. You will have some cheese? Some cold meat? Ah. Everything worth doing is worth doing to excess. There is a saying—"

"A hand in the bush is worth two on the bird," I suggested.

"I have never heard this before. I am not entirely certain I understand it in its entirety, but I can tell that there is wisdom in it."

"Thank you."

"I myself was thinking of yet another adage, but it does not matter now. I am in your debt, *kâzzih*. You have purged the world of the man who most dishonored me. Only tell me what I might do to liquidate the debt I owe you."

"Phaedra."

"Your woman."

"Yes."

"But that is less than a favor," he said. "That is merely another debt I owe. If the girl was not a slave, she was never that man's to sell. So although I may have purchased her, she was never mine to sell when I sold her, for I could not acquire a true and honest title. Do you follow me?"

"I think so."

"Thus although she may have been sold to a house of maradóosh, they cannot own her. But, because I must do business with these people, and because it was proper for them to trust me and foolish for me to trust this Englishman, the burden must fall upon me. Do you see?"

"I'm not sure."

He sighed. "But it is elementary, *kâzzih*. I shall buy the girl's freedom. If."

"Pardon."

A shadow darkened his face. "If she is alive. If you find her . . . worth taking. The men who work in the mines live in grim villages devoid of women. There are no women anywhere about except for the houses of the maradóosh. And when they receive their pay, the mine workers rush to these houses and stand in long lines to wait their turns with the slave girls. They are men of no culture, these miners. In Kabul it is a joke to call them *Yâ'ahâddashíin*. But you are a foreigner, you would not understand. It is remarkable enough that you speak our language as well as you do."

"Thank you."

"Often I can understand almost all the words you say."

"Oh."

"But these mine workers, they are crude. Rough boorish men. They use women cruelly." He lowered his head, and a tear trembled in the corner of one big blue eye. "I could not say with assurance that your woman, your girl, is alive today."

"I must find her."

"Or that you would want her. So many women, the experience ruins them. Some have in their lifetimes known only a handful of men, and then to embrace thirty or forty or fifty a day—"

"Thirty or forty or fifty!"

"Life is hard for a maradóon," Amanullah said. "There is a labor shortage."

"No wonder."

"Ah. If you will permit a delicate question, had this Phaedra considerable experience before she was brought here?"

I burned my mouth on my coffee. I barely felt the pain. I remembered a taxi racing through garbage-laden streets, a head on my shoulder, a voice at my ear. _I have things to tell you. I am Phaedra Harrow. I am eighteen years old. I am a virgin. I'm not anti-sex or frigid or a lesbian or anything. And I don't want to be seduced or talked into it. People try all the time but it's not what I want. Not now. I want to see the whole world. I want to find things out. I want to grow. I am a virgin. I am Phaedra Harrow. I am a virgin. I am eighteen years old. I am a virgin. I am a virgin. I am—_

"—a virgin," I said.

"Eh?"

"She is eighteen years old," I said. "She was never with a man in all her life."

"Extraordinary!"

"A virgin."

"Eighteen years without knowing a man!"

"Yes."

"And the likeness you showed me—she is a beauty, is it not so?"

"It may not be so now," I said. "It was so then. A beauty." I thought for a moment. "A beautiful face and body, and a beautiful spirit, my friend Amanullah."

"It is rare, this beauty of the spirit."

"Yes."

"Beauty and purity."

"Yes."

"You go to find her," he sobbed. "You take my car. My driver returns in a week's time and he drives you to look for her, to search for her."

"Search?"

"Ah, there are four houses where she might be, *kâz-zih*. Four houses scattered far apart in the vastness of Afghanistan. And I do not know to which house I sold which girls."

"Oh."

"But my driver returns in a week, and he and my car are at your disposal."

"A week," I said.

"And until then my house is your house and my refrigerator is your refrigerator."

"A week is a long time," I said. A week in Kabul, I thought, could turn out to be an exceedingly long time. That meant I wouldn't get out of the city until the 21st of the month, and the coup was scheduled for the 25th, which meant the city would be in Russian hands before I got back to it. And I would have to get back to it if I had Amanullah's car and driver along. And—

"—an excellent driver," he was saying. "A Pakistani, and when his mother lay on her deathbed, of course I told him to go to her. In a week's time he flies home from Karachi."

"He flies?"

"We have an airport in Kabul. It is most modern."

"Then the car is here."

"Of course."

"I could take it myself."

He stared at me. "You do not mean to say that you are familiar with automobiles?"

"Why, yes, I am."

"You know how to drive them?"

"Certainly."

"It is extraordinary. To think that you are able to drive automobiles. Quite extraordinary."

"Well," I said.

"Then there is no question," said Amanullah. "You leave in the morning. Now we drink beer."

Chapter Ten

❋　❋　❋

After Amanullah turned in for the night, I sat around for a couple of hours drinking fresh coffee and trying to read a local newspaper. I didn't do very well at it. An hour or so before dawn I wandered out to his garden and browsed around out there. I had suspected that a man oriented as was Amanullah would grow nothing that he couldn't eat, but I turned out to be completely wrong. The moonlight was bright enough for me to make out bed after bed of rather spectacular flowers. Some were easy enough to identify, even for a New Yorker. Others were unlike anything I had ever seen in the states.

He certainly did well for himself, I thought. The house was modern and well appointed, the garden obviously received at least one employee's full-time attention. In the Café of the Four Sisters I had not thought of him as a particularly wealthy man, but it seemed evident that he went there because he liked the cooking. Slave trading seemed highly profitable. Arthur Hook had said that he received a thousand pounds apiece for the girls, and there was no reason to doubt the figure. If Amanullah paid that sort of money, he would be likely to ask at least double that figure from the houses of maradóosh.

(This bit with the Afghan words isn't entirely to impress you with my erudition. If I wanted to do that I'd pick a language that I was better at. But maradóon is hard to translate into English. It doesn't exactly mean whore, nor does it exactly mean slave. Sort of a combination of the two, with overtones of sluttish abandon. And as for *kâz-zih*, I offer that in Afghan because I have no idea what the English for it might be. Everybody says it, but it's not in any of the dictionaries—not that there are that many English-Pushtu dictionaries to begin with. *Kâzzih* seems to be something one says to people for whom one has at least a moderately favorable regard. It is applied indiscriminately to males and females with no change in pronunciation. I do not know whether or not you address an elder as *kâzzih*; I rather think not, but I'd hate to bet money one way or the other. It might mean dear little friend, or it might mean fella, or it might mean trusted comrade. Then again, it might just as easily mean motherfucker. Work it all out for yourself, *kâzzih*.)

Well. I wandered around his garden, meditating upon the inhumanity of man to man and vice versa, and contemplating the possible profits in white slavery, and trying to think of rhymes for *maradóosh* and *Kâzzih*, and trying, in short, everything I knew of that would keep my mind off Phaedra. Nothing worked particularly well. Aside from Minna, who was really too young to count, Phaedra Harrow had been the only virgin I knew. And the thought of that frightened little child of nature being enjoyed and abused by thirty or forty or fifty men a day—

She had to be dead, I thought. Death before dishonor— no doubt that had been her credo, and my heart tore at the picture of her fighting valiantly to preserve her chastity until first that and then her very life was torn away from her.

A dreadful picture.

And yet, I thought, it was no worse than the picture of her surviving the initial assault. Because if she had to take on thirty or forty or fifty men a day, then it still amounted to the same thing. Either way she was doomed to get herself screwed to death. It was only a question of time; it might take a night or it might take a year, but the outcome, God help her, seemed preordained.

I stretched out in dewy grass. I had been on my feet for what seemed rather like forever, and it was time to let the muscles roll out and the brain go blank. The muscles weren't that much trouble. They rarely are. You take one part of your body at a time and tighten it as hard as you can, and then you let it relax all the way. You sort of work your way around your body until everything is limp, and when you tune in on yourself you can feel your muscles sort of pulsing with the coolness of it all. Some of the less voluntary muscles in the eyes and inside the head are the most common trouble spots, but if you get the technique down pat you can develop more than the usual amount of control over those muscles. This won't let you show off at parties, since the whole process is invisible, but it does mean that you can get rid of most headaches just by rearranging your head. It's easier than swallowing all that aspirin.

Blanking the mind was something else again. My mind was all knotted up and I couldn't get it to let go and relax. I found myself wondering if maybe some day I shouldn't try getting into the whole process a little deeper. Pay a visit to one of the Indian ashrams and let some guru teach me the higher path to meditation upon the verities of the cosmos. I could even take Phaedra along, for that matter. Her name, after all, had originally been Deborah Horowitz.

Still, she didn't look guruish.

I thought about that pun, and I generalized upon the confusion attendant upon the whole business of punning mentally in one language while holding a conversation in another. And I thought, too, that if I couldn't think of anything better to think about, I really ought to blank my mind, because no mind needed to be burdened with this sort of garbage. And I thought of this, and I thought of that, and I thought of the other thing, and then I thought of other other things.

And then the clown stepped on my hand.

It was a pretty strange feeling, let me tell you. I may not have blanked my mind, admittedly, but I had relaxed myself to the point where I was not overwhelmingly involved with my surroundings. So while I suppose he was walking softly on tippy-toes, I'm sure he was making some noise, however slight. But I was sufficiently out of it not to notice, and he returned the favor by not seeing me. I don't suppose he expected that there would be someone lying out on the lawn at four-thirty in the morning. That again made us even. I for my part hadn't expected that some joker would step on my hand at that hour.

What happened next happened quickly. I gave a yell and a yank, and he gave a yell and a stumble, and he fell down even as I was coming up. We spent awhile hitting each other, with him doing somewhat better at that than I was doing, until I remembered that I had a gun in my robe. I fumbled around and found it and dragged it out and started flailing away with it. I guess I hit a few nonvital parts of him first, arms and legs, because he made a lot of unhappy noises and suggested that my mother was the sort who walked around on four legs and said *woof* a lot. Then I got him on the head, which was what I had in mind all along, and the gun butt made a satisfying noise as it bounced off his thick skull, and he made a satisfying noise and he grunted and flopped to the ground, and I gave a satisfied sigh as I rolled out from under him and ran my hands over myself to find out what was broken. It turned out that nothing was, which struck me as worth another satisfied sigh, which I proceeded to utter.

Prowlers, burglars and sneak thieves. I supposed that a wealthy man like Amanullah would be often troubled by them, even in a city he had characterized as peaceful. And evidently this sneak thief had been scared witless by trodding upon my hand, because instead of running like a rabbit he had stood his ground like—well, like a cornered rabbit. And he'd fought dirty, the sonofabitch. And he had nerve calling me a sonofabitch, the sonofabitch, because it was he who was a—

Wait a minute.

"Sonofabitch" wasn't Pushtu. "Sonofabitch" was *English*.

I rolled the son of an English bitch over onto his back and got a look at his face. But I was wrong; he was a son of an Irish bitch. It was good old What's-His-Name from the boat. The one who had signed on with all those bloody Rooshians. The kid from County Mayo. And what in hell *was* his name, come to think of it?

He opened an eye.

"Come to think of it," I said, "what's your name again?"

"I knew you weren't Irish," he said. "Knew it all along, and here you are talking in your natural tones, and it's sick I am that I let myself be taken in by you." He opened the other eye. "You tricked me," he said, accusingly. "Snuck up and caught me by the heel and pulled me down without even a fare-thee-well. Hell of a thing to do, if you ask me."

"I didn't."

"Didn't what?"

"Didn't ask you," I said reasonably, I think. "Didn't sneak up on you, either. You stepped on my hand."

"I hope I bloody broke it."

Enough. "This is going to hurt you more than it hurts me," I said, and I hit him over the head again with the gun, and he went night-night. I had no sooner done this than I felt fairly stupid about it. It was a pleasure, certainly, but it didn't exactly accomplish anything. Now that I had him at a disadvantage, I should either have been giving him a message for his employers or learning information from him. Instead I had knocked him out.

I went into Amanullah's house and went absolutely crazy looking for something to tie the bastard up with. I didn't want to cut off a lamp cord or otherwise abuse my host's hospitality, and I couldn't find any wire or twine that wasn't already serving in some important capacity. I gave up and went outside again. Daly was still cold. I frisked him and found an Irish passport in the name of Brian McCarthy, a .22 automatic with a full clip in it, a billfold holding some Afghan notes and a sheaf of English and Irish pounds, a packet of Woodbines, and a condom

made in the state of New Jersey. The latter two items
seemed of no possible benefit to me, so I returned them to
his pockets.

He still didn't come to.

I broke open the .22, took the clip out and heaved it
into a bed of tiger lilies. I would wait until he woke up, I
decided, and then I would impress him with my sincerity.
This seemed more necessary than ever, because the
bastards just weren't giving up. Evidently the vulgar Bulgar
with the spade-shaped beard had not been convinced that
I was no threat to their coup. Or, if I'd made my point
with him, he'd had no luck selling it to the rest of them.

Because it was pretty obvious that Daly (or McCarthy,
or whoever he really was) had not come to Amanullah's
house to borrow a cup of sugar for his tay. He had come
to kill me, and perhaps to kill Amanullah in the bargain.

Which meant that they hadn't given up. Which meant,
too, that they had a hell of an accomplished organization
going for them, because somehow they had managed to
follow us to Amanullah's or get word of who I had met or
something. Whatever it was, they had done it, all right.

He was still out cold. I looked at him and decided that
I had never seen anyone look more unconscious.

"Wake up, you idiot," I told him, "because I'm going to
have to chase around from whorehouse to whorehouse,
and it is going to be less than a pleasure to have you idiots
trying to kill me. So wake up and I'll explain it to you all
over again."

I waited. The sky grew lighter and then the sun was
suddenly up above the horizon. I splashed cold water on
Daly. Nothing happened. I could see all of Kabul waking
up and wandering around to see me conferring with an
unconscious Irishman on Amanullah's back lawn.

I turned his head so that the sun was in his eyes. I
splashed more cold water on him.

The eyes opened.

"Bejasus," he said. "You've broken my head."

"You had it coming."

"I'm dying. Holy Mother-of-Pearl, I'm dying."

"Not really."

"I can see the fires of Hell before me."

"You nitwit," I said, "you're staring into the sun." I turned his head away. "There," I said, "Hell's out."

"Tanner."

"Good thinking."

"You're going to kill me."

"It's a tempting notion," I admitted. "But I'm going to prove my good faith to you. Here."

I held the gun by the barrel, the .22 and handed it to him. He looked at it suspiciously, then at me, then at it again.

"It's yours," I said. "I don't want it, I still have the one I took from your friend yesterday. Here, take it, it's yours."

He reached out, took the gun, pointed it at me and squeezed the trigger.

It made the sort of clicking noise that guns make when they're empty. He looked sadly at it.

"You're incorrigible," I told him, and took out the other gun and hit him over the head with it.

Chapter Eleven

❀ ❀ ❀

The four Afghanistan whorehouses were scattered about as far and wide as they could be, which, given the size of Afghanistan, was rather far indeed. One was located far to the north in the rugged Hindu Kush town of Rustak, conveniently located just a mile from the shacks where the Rustak gold miners lived. Another, not far from the Pakistan border, was some sixty miles south of Kandahar. There was no town nearby, just a group of mines which removed lignite and chromium from the earth. A third house catered to the iron ore miners in and around Shibarghan and Bâlkh, this in the north central part of the country. Finally, there was yet another house for iron ore miners (and whatever camel herdsmen had gotten out of the mood for camels and into the mood for love) in western Afghanistan, on the outskirts of Anardara.

Afghanistan is just a shade smaller than Texas. If you flattened it out it would be three or four times the size of Texas. And if you flattened it out it would also be several thousand times easier to drive from Kabul to Rustak to Kandahar to Anardara to Shibarghan.

The first leg of the trip was the easiest. When the Russians decided to build Afghanistan a road, they saw no reason to be morons about it. They built it from Kabul to Russia, which made it at least as useful to them as it was to the Afghans. In fact, come the 25th of November, I had the feeling that a lot of Afghans would be very damned sorry they had accepted that particular gift. The Trojans got a better bargain when they accepted the wooden horse.

As far as I was concerned, though, the road was a pleasure. Instead of going around the mountains, it went through them. Instead of curving wildly here and there, it went straight. Instead of bumping up and down, it lay flat. Instead of being as narrow as the alleyways in the old section of Kabul, it was as wide as the Jersey Turnpike. But it did not have nearly so many cars as the Jersey Turnpike. On the contrary, it seemed, as far as I could tell, to have no cars whatsoever except for the one I was driving.

I was driving what I will swear forever was a 1955 Chevrolet.

That morning, after I finally got Daly (or McCarthy) on his way, Amanullah showed me his car. First he gave me a big buildup, explaining he was sure I had never seen its like, that it was the fastest and most luxurious car it had ever been his privilege to own. I was expecting something impressive and was only wondering whether it would be closer in type to a Rolls Royce or a Ferrari. So we walked over to the place where he had the thing garaged, and there was this 1955 Chevy.

"Oh, fine," I said. "This won't be any problem. Had one just like it ten years ago. But yours is in really lovely shape. Of course I suppose you don't ride it that hard, and I guess there's no salt corrosion from rock salt on the pavements in winter. No. I don't suppose there would be. How recently did you have it painted? Not long ago, I'll bet. Beautiful condition. Even the upholstery—"

"*Kâzzih*, you talk but I cannot understand you."

"A fine car," I said.

"You understand its operation?"

"I do. I owned one like it ten years ago, Amanullah."

"But that is impossible. This car was made not four months ago."

I looked at him. "But that's why they called them 1955

Chevrolets," I said. "Because they were made by the Chevrolet people. In 1955. It explains the name."

"This car was made this year."

"Huh?"

"And not by these Chevrolet people, whoever they may be. This car is a Balalaika."

"Don't be absurd. A balalaika has a triangular box and three strings, and . . . oh. A Russian car."

"A triumph of Soviet technology, we are told."

"A Russian Chevy. They went and built a 1955 Chevy."

"I do not understand."

He didn't understand, eh? Well, I didn't understand what I was doing zipping through the Hindu Kush at speeds in excess of 90 kilometers an hour—which sounds more impressive than 57 miles per hour, even if it amounts to the same thing. Zipping through the Hindu Kush, that is, in a 1955 Chevrolet. Here it was, thirteen lucky years later, and the crazy Russians had invented the '55 Chevy.

It certainly does make you think. I remember a few years back shaking my head sadly when Nixon wagged his finger at Khrushchev and told him we were ahead of them in color television. But there's no getting away from the fact that the Russians do have a sort of cavalier attitude toward the whole question of consumer goods.

Though I don't suppose there's anything specifically wrong with the '55 Chevy. I had always liked mine, until the neighborhood juvenile delinquents had stolen so much of it that there was not enough left to drive. I suppose, actually, there was something I ought to be grateful for. After all, the Russians could have stolen the Tucker.

The first whorehouse was a compound of mud huts clustered together at the side of a mountain near Rustak. It took me a hard day's driving to reach it, and of course it wasn't the right one. That would have been too much to expect.

The madam was a gaunt hollow-eyed crone with a bald

spot on the top of her ancient head. I showed her the
letter from Amanullah, a letter addressed to her personally
and requesting that she assist me in locating a particular
girl. I was to be given the girl outright, and he would
reimburse her at a later date for the girl's price. Amanullah had given me four letters, one for each of the madams. This one read the letter through several times, then
wrinkled her brow at me.

"It does not say how much he pays for the girl," she
pointed out.

"He pays what you ask."

This delighted her, and I was offered food and drink
while she paraded her stable of whores past me. There
were fourteen or fifteen of them. There were Oriental girls
and Arab girls and Negro girls and European girls, and
despite their infinite variety they all looked alike.

"They all look alike," I said.

"Only if you turn them upside-down," the madam said,
and giggled lewdly.

I didn't want to turn them upside-down, or inside-out,
or anything. I only wanted to turn them down and myself
away. I had never seen such a sad-looking bunch of wom-
en in my life. They shuffled their feet as they walked, and
their eyes stared vacantly ahead, and their faces were
utterly expressionless. They looked like zombies, like the
living dead. No, they looked even worse than that; they
looked like a Tuesday afternoon Mah-Jongg group in
Massapequa.

"She is not here?" The hag fastened a hand to my arm.
"You show me picture again, *kâzzih*." I showed her the
picture again. "She is pretty, but other girls pretty too.
You pick one out, you buy her."

I started to tell her to forget it. Then I stopped and
thought it over. Amanullah had given me four individual
letters to the madams. They would not know that I was
only authorized to liberate one girl, Phaedra Harrow by
name. I could, if I chose, free a girl at each of the
whorehouses. The liberation of four whores is admittedly
a far cry from the abolition of slavery, but a journey of a

thousand miles begins with a single step, or, as an Afghan proverb of Amanullah's would put it, 'No sooner shear a camel than ride a sheep.'

So I looked at the girls again. With my luck, I thought, I would select the one girl who enjoyed being a whore. And what, I wondered would I do with three liberated prostitutes? The conventional answer, the obvious answer, somehow did not appeal to me. Nor did it entirely answer the question. What would I do with them afterward? If I simply released them in Kabul, they would either starve to death or get shipped back to the cathouses and sold all over again. If I took them to their original homes—well, maybe I could do that, but it sounded like a lot of trouble, and there was no way to be certain that they wanted to return to their original homes. If, as Amanullah had suggested, they were the daughters of slaves, they probably had no original homes in the real sense of the term. And if they had been sold into slavery by their parents, well, home was probably not the wisest place in the world to take them.

What really made up my mind, though, was that I would be sticking Amanullah for a debt he had no reason to pay. True, he was a rich man and could well afford it. True, too, that he had made money in the less than wholesome world of white-slaving and could thus be legitimately shafted by this sort of stratagem. The fact remained that Amanullah was a man of the highest ethical and moral standards, a man with a rich sense of hospitality and friendship. When I must choose between my friends, however corrupt and disreputable they may be, and strangers, however pure and innocent, I choose my friends.

The closest house to that one was the one in Shibarghan, but you couldn't get there from there. The mountains got in the way, and not even the pragmatic generosity of the Russians had led to the construction of a road from Rustak to Shibarghan. Maybe things would change after the Russians took over the country, I thought. Or maybe they would simply close down the whorehouses and let the miners work things out for themselves. In a free economy, you almost invariably find a whorehouse, wherever you have a large concentration of single men, except for places like Fire Island. But in a planned economy—well, consider the car I was driving, as far as that goes. The Soviets have never shown the proper attitude toward the whole topic of consumer goods. And hookers are consumer goods, even if some of them are pretty raw material.

It was with shining thoughts like this that I diverted myself as I drove all the way back to Kabul.

I stopped there long enough to buy gasoline. I filled the tank of the Balalaika, and I also filled the dozen or so five-gallon cans which filled the back seat and the trunk. When you start a trip in Afghanistan, you make sure that you have enough gas to get you where you're going and back again. There are no roadside gas stations in the countryside, no clean rest rooms, no free tourist information, no uniformed attendants to wipe your windshield and check your oil. No green stamps, no Tigerino cards, no chance to play Flying Aces or Dino Dollars or Sunny Bucks or any of the great American gas station games. Nor, for that matter, does Afghanistan have much in the way of lung cancer or emphysema or heart disease or air pollution.

I think they'll catch up, though. Kabul, surrounded by mountains on three sides, is a natural for smog once a sufficient degree of industrialization is reached. The mountains should sock in that rotten air as well as they do in Los Angeles.

From Kabul I took the southern route to Kandahar. The Russians had had nothing to do with this stretch of road, and I felt they were wise. I'd have preferred to have nothing to do with it myself. It was vaguely paved in that someone from the government had once dribbled a load of gravel down the middle of it. The rains had washed away most of the gravel and the rest of it was of little practical benefit, since it was right in the center of the road and the tires of the Balalaika passed on either side of it. The road twisted and dipped and swung this way and that, and periodically I would glance outside my window and see a couple of miles of nothing, pure nothing leading down to a barely visible valley below. The road had no shoulder. It just sat there alongside of the drop, and I held the car as close as I could to the wall on the other side of the road, and I tried to pretend that heights didn't bother me, and I was very careful not to look over the side of the cliff any more than I had to.

Just before Kandahar I hit table land, a high level plateau across which the road cut straight and true and flat. I stopped the car long enough to pour a can of gasoline into its tank, then put the pedal on the floor and urged the car onward.

Kandahar itself was a rather impressive city, with a population of close to 150,000. It was more uniformly modern than Kabul, more squat concrete block houses and fewer mud huts, more cars and fewer donkeys and camels, more men and even some women in western dress. I stopped for a meal, worked my way through to the southern edge of the city, and pressed on toward where the house was supposed to be.

The house was rather similar to the one in Rustak. There was a single barnlike dwelling instead of a slew of little huts, and the madam was gross rather than gaunt, with a hair-sprouting birthmark in the center of her chin and a group of four deep vertical scars in the center of her forehead. She laughed a lot. She laughed when I told her I had come from Amanullah, and she guffawed when I explained that I was intent upon purchasing a particular prostitute for my own purposes, and she chortled when I showed her the letter of guarantee from Amanullah.

She looked at Phaedra's picture and chuckled inanely to herself. The scars on her forehead wiggled like snakes. I thought of all those cathouses in novels where, if the madam really likes you, she'll haul you off to the bedroom herself instead of turning you over to one of the girls. If this madam did anything of the sort, I could see where she might alienate a hell of a lot of customers.

"I know her not," she said. "You want to look at my girls?"

"All right."

"They are many of them with men now. I call others."

She brought in a batch of them, and as the others finished with their clients she brought them in as well, and I guess that the girls were the true similarity between this cathouse and the other one. It certainly wasn't the physical plant which reminded me of the other, nor was it any shred of resemblance between the wicked witch of the north and the wicked witch of the south. It was the girls, the poor pathetic girls, black and white and yellow and tan, dull-eyed and bow-legged and lead-footed from constant and merciless screwing.

"No," I said, "I fear she is not here."

"You care for drink before you go?"

"Coffee, if you have some."

She did, so I did. It was particularly good, strong and rich, and I drank three cups of it. I stood to go, and the madam asked me if I wanted a girl.

"No," I said, "I shall wait until I find the girl I seek."

"Have one now. It is not good for a man to wait too long."

I shook my head, not in answer but to clear it of cobwebs. I had thought she meant I should buy one of her girls, but she was more interested in renting than selling.

I turned to look at those sheep-eyed, sad-faced girls. Most of them had left, returning to the long line of men waiting for service, but a few still dawdled about.

"I do not think so," I said.

"When did you last have a woman? You have not had a woman since you left Kabul."

"Well—"

"Not since Kabul," she repeated, her words an accusation. "Know you what happens when a man waits too long between women?"

She began to tell me and I tried not to listen. She was as

disheartening as an army training film on the ravages of venereal disease, and the fact that I knew she was crazy didn't help. It was one thing to know that you were hearing an old madam's tale; it was another thing to dismiss out of hand the urgent warning that one's thing would turn green and grow pimples and get smaller and smaller and then drop off entirely. I may not have believed it, but that certainly didn't mean I wanted to hear about it.

Not since Kabul?

Hell. Not since New York, I thought. There was a beginning with Julia Stokes, but a beginning, you will recall, was all it was; I had been forced to depart before I could arrive. Since then such opportunities as may have existed somehow never seemed worth the trouble. In France, in Tel Aviv, in Iraq and Iran—well, there were girls, certainly, but that's never reason enough in and of itself to get involved. Not unless one happens to be particularly in the mood. Which, what with all the worry and aggravation and all, I hadn't happened to be.

And still wasn't.

"I must go," I told the fat madam.

"You are less than a man," she taunted.

"Perhaps."

"You are a *farradóon* who would mince as a girl."

"You are a fat old lady with a face that would cause a clock to cease ticking."

"Fat!"

I raced for the car.

I drove back to Kandahar and managed to find a petrol pump. I filled the tank and the five-gallon cans once again, and I stopped at a grocery story to fill the rest of the car with food. Anardara was three hundred hard miles from Kandahar, and I had no idea how long the trip would take or what my chances might be of getting food or drink along the way. I bought hunks of flat bread and a large round cheese, and for drinking I took two dozen bottles of Coca-Cola.

Well, that was what they had. They have it everywhere. In parts of the world where the natives have never heard of America, everybody drinks Coca-Cola. Little kids in Asia and Africa start drinking the stuff before they're old enough to have their second teeth, and so it has a chance at their baby teeth first. In villages throughout the world, the first two words of English everyone learns—often the only words of English—are *Coca* and *Cola*.

So far the Russians haven't been able to invent it. Their finest spies have been unable to penetrate the iron-clad security system in Atlanta, where the Coca-Cola formula is guarded more carefully than the most precious of atomic secrets. All efforts to break it down chemically have met with utter failure. Nobody really knows what's in it.

I had some bread, I had some cheese, I drank a warm Coke.

I hit the road.

Chapter Twelve

❀ ❀ ❀

The Wicked Witch of the West had lost an eye to some loathsome disease. She had never bothered to replace it with a glass eye and did not wear a patch, either. Nor was she wearing a Hathaway shirt, which was just as well, because she would have set their image back immeasurably. Aside from the gaping, red-rimmed eye socket that glared at one, she wasn't particularly bad looking. Her body was well proportioned and her face would have been attractive.

She compensated for her relative shortage of deformities by reeking. She was the rankest-smelling female in the world, and it was not necessary for me to smell every woman on earth to make this statement. She stank; her breath was enough to curdle Coca-Cola and her flatulence suggested a lifelong diet of nothing but baked beans. I don't think she ever bathed; if she did, the Farah Rud River would have a water pollution problem.

"You come from Amanullah!" She slapped me on the back, put her mouth to my ear for a confidential whisper. I tried to do something about my nostrils. "He is my good friend," she hissed. (You couldn't hiss this in English, but the Afghan for it is full of sibilants. Don't quibble.) "My very good friend," she went on, still hissing. "Always he brings me my very best girls. So many of the maradóosh, they are not lovely, they do not please men, they bleed, they get sick, they die. Often they are diseased, and men complain later that their members have been set afire and immersed in acid. But from Amanullah I obtain always only the very finest, the milk of the milk. The best girl in this house is a girl Amanullah sold me."

"One of them," I said, "is a girl he should not have sold you. I must repurchase her."

"I do not sell my girls, *kâzzih*."

"Amanullah wishes to buy her himself. I am his agent."

"Oh?"

I showed her the letter. "You see? He will pay your price for the girl, whatever you declare your price to be. And of course you know that Amanullah is a man of his word, that his word is to be trusted."

"It is so."

"The girl is called Phaedra Harrow," I said. "Or perhaps she is called Deborah Horowitz."

"You do not know her name?"

"It is one of the two."

"But I know neither name," she said, punctuating the remark flatulently. I took an involuntary step backwards. "I give them new names when they come into my house, and they learn their new names even as they learn their new lives. The old names cease to have any importance for them. They are even buried under their new names."

"I see."

"So these names mean nothing."

I took out the photograph and showed it to her. She leaned forward expectantly and her black hair brushed at my nose. The odor that rose from it was absolutely incredible. It staggered the mind, to say nothing of the nostrils. My olfactory nerves were utterly unnerved. I winced at the stench, and the madam recoiled at the photo.

"She who is alive," she said.

One hears not merely words but the thoughts they comprise; otherwise none of us could speak nearly as quickly as we do and hope to be understood. And so what I heard her say was "She who is not alive," because it made more sense. One doesn't expect a person to look at a picture and recoil in horror at the thought that the pictured individual is alive. Our necrophilic culture may be headed in that direction, but so far it hasn't quite arrived.

So I thought she meant that Phaedra was dead.

Over a period of time people become their images, become their role in one's life. It takes a shock to remind one how one really regards various individuals. My mother, I remember, used to say in jest that I would not really appreciate her until she was gone. She was not serious; I guess the maudlin mush of this particular cliché appealed to her as a sort of verbal camp. And I had appreciated her, of course; we were quite close. But one day one of my aunts called, broken-voiced, to tell me that mother had somehow died, and it turned out that she had been right all along. I hadn't really appreciated her before, not as I did then.

I said, "The girl is dead?"

A moment's hesitation. Then, with a rush of words packaged in foul air, "Ah, yes, yes, you speak the truth, *kâzzih*. The girl is dead."

"The hell she is."

"Eh?"

" 'She who is alive,' " I said. "I missed it the first time, but you were all nervous when you saw the picture, and then you were relieved when I said she was dead. Where is she?"

"You must go, *kâzzih*."

I straightened up, glowered down at her. "Where is she? And why do you not answer me?"

"Phuc'mi."

"Not if you were the last woman on—huh?"

"Phuc'mi."

"I don't know what that means," I said. "In my own tongue, the tongue of a far-off land, it has a meaning. But I know little of Pushtu, and the word you speak is unknown to me."

"It is unknown to me also, *kâzzih*. It is the name of the one you seek, of She who is alive."

"Her name is Phaedra."

"Her new name. We gave it to her because it is all she says. 'Phuc'mi, Phuc'mi,' it is all she says, night and day. We try to teach her our own tongue but she refuses to learn it. One can make her learn nothing. But *kâzzih*, I will tell you this. She is the best maradóon ever to work in this house. She is the finest worker I have ever had."

"No," I said.

"The finest in all my years. Her beauty is greater than the others. I noticed this when she came to me, but what did it matter? A few weeks and all my girls lose their beauty. These miners and camel herders, what know they of beauty? When they have no money for maradóosh they content themselves in the orifices of their camels."

"I suppose it's better than riding one," I said.

"But this Phuc'mi," she said. "That which makes other girls grow pale and wither, makes her grow ever more beautiful. That which puts death in the eyes of the others gives her eyes the spark and sparkle of life. And with men she is wild. She can please a man as can no other girl I have ever known."

"No," I said.

"But it is so."

I shook my head wordlessly. Not Phaedra, I thought. Not my little virgin, not my cloistered nun. It was patently impossible. Mother Horowitz's little girl was not the sort to reign as star performer in an Afghanistan whorehouse. Mother Horowitz's beloved Deborah wasn't the possessor of the camel herders' favorite orifice. I could, like the Red Queen, believe six impossible things before breakfast. This, though, I simply could not believe.

"And so we call her 'She who is alive,' " the smelly old pig was saying. "Because that which brings others to their death gives her more and more of life, so that she thrives upon it and grows every day younger and fairer. She is my jewel, *kâzzih*, my treasure, the flower of my garden." It was an obscenity for anything that smelled like this even to speak of flowers and gardens. *She is the cabbage of my skunk,* maybe. *She is the arm of my pit,* even. But farther than that one could not go.

"And so I cannot let her go," she said.

"But that's ridiculous."

"She is worth more than any three of my girls combined. She can go with more men in a night than the others, and the men prefer her, they wait in a long line for her. I thought that if they want her more, then they should pay more for her, and so I raised her price. Thirty for the other girls, fifty for Phuc'mi. They pay her price. They stand in line for her. She is the queen of this house of maradóosh."

"She does not belong here."

"But she does."

"She belongs in her own country," I said. "With her own mother, and with the ones who love her. She—"

The hog bristled. "You say that we do not love her? I, who could not care for her more were she my own daughter? She reminds me of my own self in my youth." This I rather doubted. "And the other girls, do you think they do not care for Phuc'mi? They regard her as their sister. And do you not think the men care for her? Would they pay such prices for one for whom they do not care?"

I turned from her, went outside for a moment. I wanted some fresh air, not just to clear my nose but to clear my head as well. I looked out over the desolate landscape. It was the middle of the afternoon and most of the girls were sleeping. Soon they would awaken and have their breakfast. Shortly thereafter the men would arrive from their camels, from the mines. And Phuc'mi-Phaedra-Deborah would have her work cut out for her until sunrise.

I went inside again. I told the foul-smelling old woman that, when all was said and done, she had no real choice in the matter. Amanullah would pay her price, whatever it might turn out to be. If the girl was worth that much, Amanullah would nevertheless make it good. Her customers might be unhappy, but she did hold the whip hand; after all, her house was the only game in town, and if it came down to a choice between her girls and camels, well, it might be close but her girls would surely carry the day. However good an adjustment Phaedra might have made to

Afghanistanian whoredom, she surely belonged in her own home.

And, as a final argument, I showed her the gun. I explained that if she did not deliver Phaedra at once I would shoot her, and then I would go through the house and shoot all the other girls, and then I would take Phaedra away anyhow. This was sheer bravado, since the gun didn't have that many bullets in it anyway, and since I wouldn't have gone around shooting innocent maradóosh to begin with, but I guess she believed enough of it to go get Phaedra. She choked back a sob and said something which must have been interestingly obscene, some suggestion no doubt as to the ideal employment for diverse portions of my anatomy. And then she went away.

I steeled myself. Well, aluminumed myself, anyway. I told myself Phaedra was going to look like hell, and might be more than a little hysterical, and would need no end of tender loving care.

Whereupon she appeared.

She was more beautiful than could be believed. I use the awkward construction purposefully; "unbelievably beautiful" is one of those clichés fastened on every sunset and most Swedish films, the latter of which are at best believably beautiful. Phaedra was something quite out of the ordinary. I have already told you what she looked like, and she still looked that way, but with a new radiance, a special glow, a lilt to her walk and to her smile that had not been there before.

Before she had been a beautiful virgin. Now she was as beautiful as ever, and she wasn't exactly a virgin any more. She was, from what I had heard, as far from the state of virginity as she and I both were from the state of New Mexico, and perhaps even farther than that.

"Phaedra," I said.

"Phuc'mi," she said.

"Phaedra, it's me. Evan. Evan Tanner. From New York. You remember me, Phaedra."

"Phuc'mi."

"And your name is Phaedra Harrow. Once your name

was Deborah Horowitz. Do you remember? And then you changed it to Phaedra, and then——"

"Phuc'mi."

She was wearing a piece of silk that was sort of wrapped all over her and fastened at the shoulder. Purple silk. She said her new name a few more times, and then she unfastened the purple silk and unwrapped herself like a self-opening Christmas present, and I looked at the glory that had lived untouched with me in New York, and the same glory that had since turned on half the camel schleppers in Afghanistan, and I think I got a little weak in the knees.

"She wishes not to go with you," said the "before" half of the Ban ad. "She wishes only to stay here. I do not think she understands what you say to her."

She was right. Phaedra's eyes gave the show away. They had the queer light of madness in them. I nodded and went out to the car. I came back with a bottle of Coke.

"Coca-Cola," said Phaedra.

"She is mad for Coca-Cola," said the madam. "There is an empty bottle she takes every morning to sleep with her."

"She used to like wine," I recalled. "But she wasn't queer for the bottles." I opened the Coke and gave it to Phaedra and turned to go back for another one.

"Get two," the madam said.

I didn't want to. I knew it would make her belch, and I could imagine what that would smell like. But I got two more Cokes, and we all three drank ours down. I was the first to finish. I waited patiently until Phaedra was through with hers. She put the bottle down and gave me her one response to life, saying the new name by which she was so well known in the area.

And I hit her over the head with the Coke bottle.

"My head hurts," she said.

"You're awake."

"You hit me."

I took my eyes off the road and looked at her. She looked better than ever, but the madness had not left her eyes. I put my eyes back on the road just in time to avoid putting the car off the road, and I agreed that I had hit her, by George.

"What with?"

"A Coke bottle."

"Oh. Stop the car, Evan."

"You know who I am."

"Sure. I knew back there but I couldn't talk. I couldn't say anything, just what I said over and over. I get blocked all the time, I can't even think. Stop the car."

"What for?"

"Just do it."

I stopped the car, and Phaedra came into my arms and unzipped my fly.

"Hey," I said.

"What's the matter?"

"Well, I don't know."

"You always wanted to. From the first time you saw me you wanted to. Always. But I wouldn't let you. I wouldn't let anybody. They didn't care that I wouldn't let them, not here. I couldn't even tell them. I couldn't tell anybody anything because they didn't know what the hell I was talking about. They said things I didn't understand, and they didn't understand anything I said, and it was horrible. Why isn't it hard?"

"What?"

"Your thing. I want it hard so that we can do it. Don't you want me?"

"Of course, but—"

"I know how to get it hard. Just a minute."

But I was gently pushing her away. I held her at arm's length, and she looked unhappily at me and wanted to know what was the matter.

"You don't want me."

"Sure, but—"

"The hell you do. I want to go back there. It was nice there. I got as much as I wanted. All night long, practically. As soon as one was finished another one would come. They didn't want to talk or anything. All they wanted to do was—"

"I know, I know."

"How come you don't want to, Evan?"

I looked into her poor insane eyes. She was so magnificently beautiful it was almost painful to look at her, and she was begging me to do more than look, and she might as well have asked me to swim the English Channel.

Come to think of it, that's a rotten metaphor. I had already swum the English Channel. And I had crossed the burning deserts and, in the Hindu Kush, had driven through some of the tallest mountains, even if I hadn't literally climbed them. I'd performed all the proper Herculean tasks, all for love of a girl named Phaedra, and the only thing left was to claim my prize.

And I certainly couldn't do that.

Because this wasn't Phaedra. This was a poor sick kid with her sweetness and charm temporarily (one hoped) buried under a sea of nymphomaniacal hysteria. This was not something one took to bed, no matter how much she asked one to.

In the first place, I got a little sick at the thought of it. It seemed indecent. If I hadn't known her before it might have been different, but I had, and it wasn't.

And in the second place, even if I had managed to rationalize the first place, the whole thing would have been roughly akin, in a purely physical sense, to the prospect of inserting a boiled noodle in a bouncing bagel. Not quite impossible, perhaps, but not bloody likely either.

She said, "I thought you were my friend."

"I am."

"Is something wrong with me?"

"No."

"Then is something wrong with you?"

"I don't think so."

"Then what's the matter, Evan?"

"You're not you," I said.

"I don't get you."

"That's the idea."

"Huh?"

I pulled the car onto the road. Phaedra, rejected, hurt, cringed against the door on the passenger side. I drove for a little while and didn't say anything. She announced that she was going to take a nap. I told her it sounded like a good idea. She pouted and said that she couldn't take a nap because she was sexually frustrated. I told her to play with herself. She said that sounded like a fine idea, and she proceeded to do just that, while I proceeded to pay more attention to the road than the road really deserved. Finally she gave up and told me that it wasn't the same at all. "I'm going to sleep now," she said, and did.

When she woke up she was worse. She could barely talk at all, and she couldn't keep her hands off me. This might have been somewhat more flattering if she had not been so obviously out of her mind. She would let loose with a wild peal of laughter, then make a grab at my groin, then burst just as suddenly into tears.

A little of this goes a long way. A lot of it, which is what I was getting, goes even further. I wanted very much to do something that would at least render her unconscious for a time, but I couldn't quite bring myself to hit her again. I didn't want to hurt her. She was more to be pitied than censured, just as her language was more to be pitied than censured. The only thing wrong with pity as an emotion is that it's so goddamned tiresome. It bores the subject and does nothing for the object.

I drove on, doing my best to ignore her. She was as easy to ignore as an earthquake, and about as subtle. But I kept the car on what the map laughingly called a road— a new one this time, a more direct route from Anardara right through to Kabul, bypassing Kandahar and presumably cutting quite a few miles off our journey. This road was what I kept my eyes on, which was something of a waste, actually, since in most places the road was so narrow that one could have covered it adequately, leaving the other eye free to do what it wanted. Since there was nothing else it wanted to do, I kept my eyes, both of them, on the road, as I guess I may already have said, and while doing this little thing I concentrated on figuring out what to do after I got back to Kabul.

I had to take her some place where they could do something for her. That much was obvious. Some place quite and restful and eminently sane. Those qualifications gave me three reasons for ruling out the place I had originally assumed we would go, since New York was neither quiet nor restful nor sane, and never will be. In New York all I could do would be to turn her over to an analyst, which would involve paying around thirty dollars an hour for a period of several years to establish that Mrs. Horowitz had discouraged little Debbie from smearing her fecal matter on the wall. I could think of many things for which to blame Mrs. Horowitz, but this was not one of them, and I couldn't see any reason to spend thirty dollars an hour for revelations of this nature.

Or else we could go back to Switzerland. They have a thing there called the Sleep Cure, and I supposed that Phaedra could take it. They just keep you asleep almost forever and let your unconscious work things out on its own. You get better, the idea seems to be, but because you are asleep during it all your conscious mind doesn't know that you're better. So you go on being the same old lunatic, but deep down inside you're sane.

I may have that wrong. Somehow, though, my own personal situation is such that I'm illogically biased against anything called the Sleep Cure. *Mea culpa*, perhaps, but *sic friat crustulum.*

Oh.

About seventy miles out of Anardara, I knew where I would take her.

And about ninety miles out of Anardara, the helicopter opened fire on us.

Chapter Thirteen

❀   ❀   ❀

At first I didn't know what the hell it was. I heard a droning noise, but the chopper was overhead to our rear and I didn't see it. Then there was a rattling noise. Puffs of dirt dug a line across the road in front of us. I hit the brake, and the helicopter hovered into view up ahead, and another blast of automatic weapon fire dug up the road.

Phaedra's eyes were wide open. "What the hell is that?"

"A helicopter. Out of the car. Fast."

"But—"

"They're trying to kill us."

"Why?"

"I don't know," I said. "Get out of the car and make it quick. Open your door. That's right. Now go for the ditch—no, wait, give them a minute to swing across to the other side. Jump for the ditch when I tell you. . . . Okay, now!"

She made a half-hearted leap for the ditch. I sprang out after her and goosed her along, and we wound up in the ditch by the side of the road. She started to straighten up. I grabbed hold of her, pulled her down.

"It smells in here," she said.

We were calf-deep in water, and she was right; it smelled. I guess it was some sort of drainage ditch, but that didn't make sense because the area we were passing through was relatively arid. From the aroma it could have been a sewer, except that this was an even more ridiculous notion. We were in the middle of nowhere, with no towns or villages nearby, let alone a city large enough to have sewers. I decided it was just one of those great underground springs that happened to surface. But instead of being a pure, clean, cold underground spring, this one stank like a sewer.

"What are they doing, Evan?"

"Circling."

"Why?"

"To make another pass at us."

"They want to make a pass at us?"

"Not that kind of a pass. They want to zoom in on us and shoot the hell out of us."

"Why?"

"I don't know."

"Are they friends of yours?"

"That's the stupidest question I've ever heard in my life."

"I mean do you know who they are?"

"No."

"Well, you don't have to bite my head off."

"Yes."

"You do?"

"I mean yes, I know who they are," I said.

"You just said you didn't."

"I just saw them again. Those crazy sons of bitches."

"Who are they?"

"Some Russians. Some crazy, cockeyed Russians. They tried to drown me and shoot me and stab me and poison me and explode me. They're the most hostile bastards imaginable. Oh, great."

"What?"

"They know we got out of the car."

"Well, of course they do. They're not blind."

"I guess not." I had the gun out, the butt cozy in my hand, the trigger firm beneath my forefinger. It was reassuring and all that, but I didn't see what in hell I could possibly accomplish with it. It is possible to bring down a helicopter with a rifle, if you're a good shot and a lucky person. With a pistol, the only way to manage it is to be flying in the helicopter at the time and to shoot the pilot. Even then it's a chancy operation at best.

Phaedra started to straighten up. I got a hand on her shoulder and shoved her down again. Her purple silk thing came unglued and began to unwind itself from her flesh. She began to breathe faster, and I turned to her and saw the light glinting wildly in her eyes.

"For Christ's sake," I said.

"I can't help it."

"I mean there's a time and a place for everything—"

"We had time before. And a place."

"Honey—"

"You just don't love me at all!"

"Then what am I doing in Afghanistan?"

"Getting us all killed."

I clenched my teeth. The cruddy little helicopter was hovering all over the place now, buzzing here and there, loosing experimental bursts of gunfire hither and yon. The man flying the thing looked vaguely familiar, and I guessed that I had seen him before on the boat across the Channel, although I couldn't place him precisely. The joker with the Bren gun—I think that's what it was, but I wasn't quite close enough to be sure—was my old Bulgarian buddy with the black spade-shaped beard.

"Why do they want to kill us, Evan?"

"They want to kill me. They don't care about you."

"Why?"

"Because they never even heard of you."

"I mean, why do they want to kill you?"

"Because they're idiots," I said. "They know that I know that they plan to overthrow the government of Afghanistan in a couple of days. What they don't know, although I keep trying to tell them, is that I don't give a damn what they do with the government of Afghanistan as long as you and I can get out of the goddamned country first. But they won't—I could shoot them now."

"Why don't you?"

I braced my elbow against the side of my body, rested my gun hand on the rim of the ditch. They were hovering directly across the road from us, with the Bulgarian spraying the ditch on that side with Bren-gun fire. I drew a bead on the pilot and let my finger tighten up on the trigger.

"No," I said, and lowered the gun.

"Oh, Evan. I know it's immoral to kill, but—"

"Immoral to kill?" I stared at her. "Are you out of your mind? Killing those sons of bitches is the most moral thing I can think of."

"Then—"

"But if they don't go back and tell their boss that they accomplished their mission, he'll know we're still alive. He'll know I'm still alive, that is. And he'll send more clowns after us, and maybe next time we won't get out of the car in time. But if we let them go home—"

"They'll tell their boss that they couldn't get us."

I shook my head. "Not likely. Nobody likes to run home boasting about a failure. They'll figure they got us in that ditch. Watch—here they go, up, up and away."

I was two-thirds right. They went up, and they went up. And then the nose of the Bren gun appeared over the side of the chopper, and a burst of bullets descended, headed for the trunk and gas tank of the 1968 Balalaika sedan.

I grabbed Phaedra and pulled her down flat in the ditch. Filthy water soaked my robes, coursed all over her naked body. She said something, but I never learned what it was, because the sound of the exploding car drowned it out.

"You should have shot them when you had the chance, Evan."

"I know."

"Because we'll never get out of here now."

"I know."

"I mean, I'm not very good at walking. And it's sort of chilly now, and when it gets dark—"

"I know."

"I don't mean to complain, Evan."

"Then shut up," I explained.

But she was right about one thing. It was silly to keep on walking. All we would accomplish would be to deplete our energy. We were, according to my calculations, something like 375 miles from Kabul. If we walked twelve hours out of twenty-four, and if we managed four miles an hour, it would take us eight days to get to Kabul. This was the mathematical solution, and one of the drawbacks of mathematical analysis is that it doesn't take everything into consideration. It was possible, for instance, that Phaedra could sustain this pace the first day. It was even possible that she could manage it the second. But while she might be able to travel 48 miles in one day and 96 miles in two, it was quite inconceivable that she could go 375 miles in eight days.

Which meant that walking was a waste of time.

So we sat down. It was twilight, and getting darker fast, and already the air had turned perceptibly colder. We were wearing the same clothing as before, having let the dying sun dry my robe and Phaedra's silk thing before we left the burned-out Balalaika and struck off down the road. I put an arm around her now, and we huddled together for warmth and comfort, and it was a tender moment, and then I felt a small warm hand insinuate itself beneath my robe.

"No," I said.

The hand went away and she began to cry. I hugged her and told her that everything would be all right. "I hate myself when I'm like this," she said between sobs. "But I can't help it."

"You'll be all right."

"My head gets all strange and I can't think of anything else. Sometimes I think I never existed before that place. That whorehouse. That I just suddenly happened there one day, that before then I was never even alive."

"You were alive."

"I was?"

"Uh-huh. You'll be alive again."

"I will?"

"Uh-huh."

"I'm afraid, Evan."

"Don't be afraid."

"We'll die on this fucking road. We'll freeze to death or starve. I'm hungry already."

"We'll be all right."

"How can you be sure?"

So I gave her a little sermon about the earth, and how one defeats oneself by expecting the land to be hostile. It isn't. There is a modern tendency to suspect that human beings cannot possibly stay alive in any area that is not paved. But one must remember that mankind did not evolve in cities, that cities were a creation of man and not the other way around. There was a time, I told her, when human beings were not terrified at the prospect of breathing air they couldn't see. There was a time when men and women ate food without first defrosting it. There was a time—

"Evan."

"What is it?"

"I'm afraid."

"Lie down. Close your eyes. Sleep."

"I can't possibly sleep."

"Lie down. Close your eyes."

"I'm wide awake. I can't—"

While she slept, I took a stick and scratched in the sand. I had left Kabul on the morning of the 15th of November, just midway between Guy Fawkes Day and the scheduled Russian coup. Since then, day and night had had a way of merging together, with too much time passed in a blur on the road, but I was able to work it out a little at a time. As well as I could determine, it was now the evening of the 21st. We had something like four days to get back to Kabul and shake things up.

Because, dammit, they had it coming now. I had given them every chance on earth, every possible chance, and they blew it over and over again. All they had had to do was leave me alone, that was all. I kept catching them and letting them go in munificent gestures of good will, and all they did was go back and organize fresh attempts on my life.

Well, they had gone too far. I was a patient man, but patience has a limit, and my limit had been reached and surpassed. A dagger in my turban, poison in my drink, a gun in my face, a bomb in my restaurant, a foot on my hand—I had contented myself for too great a time with passive resistance. Nonviolence is a marvelous concept, but it can be carried too far.

I've always like Glenn Ford movies. Especially the really lousy ones, where he's a cop that the crime syndicate is after or a sheepman that the cattlemen are after, and they keep doing mean things to him. They hit him, and they roll him along a piece of barbed wire, and they shove dynamite up his nose, and they throw him in the creek, and they poison his well, and they spill hot coffee on him, and throughout all of this Glenn Ford shows his first expression—*irritation*.

Then they go too far. They blow up his wife and kids, or they insult his mother, or they step on his blue suede shoes. Whatever it is, it's the straw, man, and Glenn Ford is the camel's back, and that does it. At this point he shows his second expression—*aggravation*.

And he goes berserk and knocks the hell out of every last one of the bastards.

I'd been irritated ever since I swam the English Channel.

I was now aggravated, and they were in trouble.

Chapter Fourteen

❀ ❀ ❀

*We reached Kabul two hours after dawn on the morn-*ing of November 24th. We rode trimphantly into town, I with a sash around my neck and a rifle over my shoulder and a pistol on my hip, Phaedra wearing men's clothing and carrying a British Army canteen and a German pistol. I pulled up on the reins and our horse neighed gratefully and went down to his knees. We dismounted. The horse stayed on his knees. I didn't really blame him, and I was surprised he hadn't dropped dead altogether.

We had stolen the horse. According to family legend, a great-great-uncle had done much the same thing in the Wyoming Territory, and had subsequently become, as far as I know, the only Tanner ever hanged in the Western Hemisphere. That sort of skeleton in the ancestral cupboard makes one a bit apprehensive about stealing horses, but the clown to whom the horse had belonged had really left us no choice.

He stopped at our signal, a tall slim Afghan who carried himself with military bearing. His moustache bristled, his eyes bored into mine. I told him I wanted to buy his horse. He said that the animal was not for sale. I told him I would pay its price in gold several times over. He said that he had no use for gold and much use for the horse. I told him I would pay equally for a ride to Kabul. He said that he was going only so far as his village a few miles away. I suggested that I might borrow the horse, and that I would leave it for him to reclaim in Kabul, and that I would pay him enough gold to make his troubles worthwhile. He remarked that, if he wanted my gold, he could simply return for it when my woman and I had perished of thirst.

So I took out the gun and told him to get off the horse or I would shoot him dead. He took told of his rifle, and I squeezed the trigger of the handgun and nicked his earlobe. He touched it with his finger, looked at the bead of blood on his fingertip, and respectfully dismounted from the horse.

"You are a superb marksman, *kâzzih*," he said. "My steed is yours."

So were his rifle and his clothing. I forebore telling him that I was not a superb marksman at all. I had not been aiming for his earlobe. I had been aiming for the center of his forehead, because when someone draws a rifle to shoot me with I want to do more than scare him a little. My rotten shooting was his good fortune.

It turned out that Phaedra had never been on a horse before. I had her ride sidesaddle at first, but after a few miles of jogging along she swung her leg over the horse. I was right behind her and I watched her, and after a few minutes I figured out what she had in mind. She would start to breath a little faster than normal, and as the horse bounced she would bounce along with it, and muscles worked in her thighs, and she made odd little noises deep in her throat, and then, finally, she would give a little sigh and fall forward, her arms around the horse's neck.

She kept doing this.

Once we were in the city we got off the poor goddamned horse and sort of abandoned him. I suppose it's not good policy to abandon horses, and there's probably a local ordinance against it, but abandoning a horse can't be any worse than stealing it in the first place, and I had a hunch that whoever took over the horse's ownership would do at least as good a job as we had done. As far as

I was concerned, if I never saw a horse again it would be fine. I had what are probably called saddle sores, except that this particular horse had not had a saddle, so I guess what I had were bareback sores, if there is such a thing. There was such a thing as far as I was concerned. I staggered along, cross-eyed and bowlegged and wholly out of sorts. Phaedra, too, looked a little bowlegged, but I don't know whether that was caused by the horse or by the way she had spent the past two months in Anardara. Bowleggedness is an occupational disease of maradóosh.

"I'm going to miss that horse," she told me, on the way to Amanullah's house.

"I can believe it."

"I never realized the rapport a human being and a horse can establish."

"Yeah, rapport."

"I mean—"

"I know what you mean."

"Evan, I can't help it."

"I know."

"I just have to—"

"I know."

"You always wanted me. In New York, in your apartment—"

"Yeah, I remember."

"I just—"

"Forget it."

"Maybe I should kill myself."

"Yeah, kill yourself."

"Evan, do you mean that?"

"Huh?" I snapped to attention. "No," I said. "No, my mind must have been wandering. Don't kill yourself. Everything'll be all right. Believe me. Everything will be all right."

"But you don't want me. You came halfway around the world to save my life and now you don't even want me any more."

"I'll get over it."

"You hate me."

"Oh, hell. I don't hate you."

"You must. You came all the way to Afghanistan to save me from a fate worse than death and now you find out that I'm actually a whore at heart. Aren't I?"

"No."

"But I am," she wailed.

I turned on her. "Now shut up for a minute," I roared. "This goddamned city is absolutely crawling with a bunch of crazy Russians. Crazy, murdering Russians. And I only know one man in the whole damned city, and he's the man who gave me that car. It was his car and he was very proud of it, and he loaned it to me and now it's gone. And I have to tell him the car is gone, and that he'll never see it again—"

"Why do you have to tell him?"

"Shut up. I have to tell him this, and then I have to get him so mad at the Russians that he'll get the rest of the city equally mad at them. And then between the two of us, Amanullah and I have to lead mobs to root out the stupid Russians and hang them from the street lamps, and I have a feeling that there are more Russians than street-lamps in this crazy city. And I have to do all this without getting killed, and without getting you killed, and then the two of us have to get the hell out of here. Do you understand what I'm talking about?"

"I guess so."

"And do you understand why I have more important things on my mind than your twat?"

"I—"

"Come on."

Amanullah was not at his house. We found him at the Café of the Seven Sisters. He was eating a leg of lamb.

I told him the whole story while he ate, and it hit home with such force he almost stopped eating. As it was, he quit while there was still a little meat clinging to the bone. He pounded the bone down on the top of the table and roared. Every eye in the place was on him.

"To attempt to destroy our country is an outrage," he bellowed.

A murmur ran through the crowd.

"To attempt the assassination of my young friend and his woman is barbarism," he cried out.

The crowd surged forward, muttering agreement, adding shouts of encouragement.

"But to destroy my automobile," Amanullah screamed. *"To destroy my automobile,"* he shrieked. "MY AUTO-MOBILE!"

The crowd was roaring its agreement.

"Twenty miles to the gallon," Amanullah bawled.

The crowd pressed at the doors of the cafe.

"Automatic transmission! You never had to shift!"

The crowd was in the streets.

"Snow tires!"

The crowd was adding new members. Lurking in the shadows I saw the Bulgarian with the pointed beard. "It's one of them," I called out, "Don't let him get away!"

They didn't let him get away. Men and women, screaming hysterically, took hold of his arms and legs and tore him apart. Little children used his head for a soccer ball. And the crowd, wild with the taste of blood, surged down the street toward the Soviet Embassy.

"Vinyl seat covers," Amanullah screamed. *"A heater! A radio! An emergency brake! Oh, the villains!"*

The Afghan police, reinforced by soldiers, took to the streets. They flooded the area around the Soviet Embassy. There were whispered exchanges between the police and the crowd.

The police joined the crowd.

The army joined the crowd.

"Onward," shouted Amanullah. "For Kabul! For Afghanistan! For your lives and your country and your sacred honor! *For my car!*"

Those poor goddamned Russians.

Chapter Fifteen

❀   ❀   ❀

I sat cross-legged on the ground. I was wearing a white loin cloth and holding, in both hands, a yellow flower. I did not know the name of the flower. I knew that names were but an illusion, and that what one must seek to know is not the name of the flower but the essence of the flower, the flowerness of the flower, and through it the flowerness of oneself and the selfness of the universe. And I poured the selfness of myself into the flowerness of the flower, and time opened and flowed like wine, and I was the flower and the flower was I.

The Manishtana sat cross-legged beside me. I handed him the flower. He looked deep into its center and said nothing for a long time. He returned the flower to me. I looked at it some more.

"You meditate," he said.

"Yes."

"It is beauty, the flower, and you meditate upon it in the peace of the ashram, and you sense the beauty, and it becomes a part of you as you in turn become a part of it. And there are three parts to the beauty. There is the beauty that exists and is perceived, and there is the beauty that exists but is not perceived, and there is the beauty that is perceived but does not exist."

I studied the flower.

"You meditate, and your mind recovers."

"It does."

"You regain health."

"I am much better. I have stopped vomiting."

"That is good."

"I can concentrate again. And I no longer break out in cold sweats all the time."

"But you do not sleep," said the Manishtana.

"No."

"So you have not yet healed yourself."

"I do not think that is to be healed."

"Man is to sleep. There is the night that is for sleep and the day that is for wakefulness, and there is no time between the two, just as the Holinesses in their infinite wisdom give us no state between wakefulness and sleep, or between yin and yang, or man and woman, or good and evil. It is the principle of dualism."

"It is my special difficulty," I said. "I was wounded long ago in a forgotten war. The powers of light took the art of sleep from me, and they alone can return it."

"The perfect man sleeps of night," said the Manishtana.

"Nobody's perfect," I said.

I found Phaedra sitting in the garden beside the waterfall. She was smelling a flower. She had her eyes closed, and she was curled up in the foetal posture clutching the flower in both hands. She had her nose in it and she seemed to be trying to inhale it.

"Good day," I said.

"I am a flower, Evan. And the flower is a girl named Phaedra."

"The beauty is the flower and the beauty is the girl."

"You, too, are beautiful."

"We are all flowers who would be as flowers."

"I love you, Evan."

"I love you, Phaedra."

"I am better now."

"And I, too."

"We both talk funny. We talk like the Manishtana. We

speak strangely, and converse of flowers, and the beautiness of things, and the wonderfulness and flowerness of our holy souls."

"We do."

"But we are well again." She sat up, crossed one leg over the other. "Evan, I know what happened in that other country. I was with men, many men every day, day after day. I know this, but I cannot recall it."

"This is your good fortune."

"Evan, I know that I enjoyed it, that it was a sickness with me, and that I was so sick and so dominated by the yang of all, that you were sick at the touch of me. I know this, but I remember it not."

"There are those parts of the lifeness of life which we must know but not remember, and there are those parts of the lifeness of life which we must remember but need not know."

"The Manishtana told me that yesterday. Or something like it. There are times when I think that it does not matter what the Manishtana says, but only that it sounds well to one's ears."

"It is so with all of human speech. What one says is of less matter than the vibrations of the sounds one utters."

"Evan, I am at peace again."

I kissed her. Her mouth was honey and spice and cider and flowers and the songs of small birds and the purring of kittens and the petals of a rose. Her sighing was the wind in the trees and rain on a snug roof and flames on a hearth. Her skin was velvet and wool and cotton and satin and bedsheets and blankets and fur. Her flesh was food and water. Her body was my body and my body was her body, and thunder rolled in the hills and bolts of lightning skipped like rams.

"Ah," she said.

Her body was my body and my body was her body, yin and yang, darkness and light, east and west. Hare krishna Hare krishna. Hare rama Hare rama. The twain shall meet.

Om.

"Never before," said Phaedra Harrow.

A bead of sweat trickled down her golden breast. I flicked at it with my tongue. She purred. I flicked at other nonexistent beads of sweat. She giggled and purred some more.

"Never before," she said again. "I thought I was all better a few minutes ago, and it turns out I didn't even know what all better was. Do you know what I mean?"

"Do I ever."

"I don't even have to talk like the Manishtana any more. That was sort of fun, but I can see where it might get to be a hangup. I mean, flowers are very nice."

"Flowers are wonderful."

"But you could get kind of dragged with doing nothing but grooving on flowers all day."

"True."

I put an arm around her and drew her close. Her mouth opened for my kiss. We held each other for a moment.

"Evan? Just now. It was really something."

"You don't have to talk about it."

"I know. I sort of want to. But I don't know the words."

"Forget it. There aren't any."

"In Afghanistan. That whorehouse. It never happened."

"I know."

"I was never there. My body was there but my soul left my body. It was off somewhere, frozen in ice."

"It's not frozen now."

"Oh, no. Oh, that feels good."

"Uh-huh."

"You do love me, don't you?"

"Of course."

"How nice. Oh, that feels wonderful!"

"Ah."

"Three steps to enlightenment," said the Manishtana. "Three branches of the trinity. Three parts of time, past and present and future. Yesterday and today and tomorrow."

"Ah."

"Three precepts of the sanctity of the ashram. Piety and Poverty and Chastity."

"We are pious," I said.

"This is true."

"And pover— And poor."

"Yes. You gave over all of your gold to the ashram upon arriving. Yes, it is so."

"Uh, the other thing. Well."

"Yes," said the Manishtana. His eyes seemed for a moment to twinkle in his wrinkled little head, but it was hard to be certain. He plucked a flower, inhaled it with his eyes. "Yes," he said.

"Two out of three," I said, "isn't all that bad an average."

"Many of the supplicants at the ashram violate the precept of chastity," he said.

"Well, exactly my point. Uh—"

"But not so often."

"Well—"

"Rarely in the daytime."

"Oh."

"Never in the flower beds."

"Uh."

The Manishtana plucked another flower. "When you came here," he said to me, "you could not blank your mind, you could not relax your hold upon the inner workings of yourself, you could not find peace, you could not relate to the unity, the oneness of self, the selfness of one."

"True."

"And now?"

"Now I no longer have this problem, Manishtana."

"And you can meditate?"

"Yes."

"And you cling to the mantra which I have given unto you?"

"I do."

"Ah," said the Manishtana. "And you, Phaedra. When you came first to the ashram, you were not yourself. Your mind had gone from your body, and in your body was a demon, and the demon drove you. And before the demon, before there was ever a demon within you, then there was ice and coldness, and even in the days before the demon you were not yourself. It is so?"

"It is so," Phaedra said.

"And now the demon has departed, you have thought him away and felt him away and meditated beyond the powers of demonness and deviltry, and yet the ice is also gone, and you are yourself. It is so?"

"It is."

"Then it is time. You may go now."

"To meditate?"

He shook his head. "To America."

"But we don't have any money," Phaedra said, "and we don't know anyone around here, and all we have are these dumb clothes, and we have to leave the ashram. I don't know what we're going to do."

"We're going to make love," I said.

"But after that."

"You heard the man. We're going home."

"How?"

"We shall find a way. Rejoice in the nowness of now. You are no longer a virgin and no longer a nymphomaniac. Instead you have retained the more desirable aspects of each facet of the youness of you. The thouness of thou."

"The essence of ess."

"The royal highness of royal high."

"The finesse of fi."

"Let's make love right over there. Right in the middle of all those fucking flowers."

"He'll throw us out."

"He already threw us out."

"Oh. Let's, then."

In the private jet of that famous recording group, the

Cock-A-Roatches, Lloyd Jenkins took a deep drag on a brown cigarette, inhaled deeply, and spent a few moments smelling a flower that wasn't, as far as I could tell, there.

"What I say," he said, "is if you can't ball a bird when you've a mind to, what's the point in meditating?"

"A point."

"So when we saw the two of you, you know, and then that holy man went at you like that, why I thought to myself, here he is, driving them out of the Garden of Eden when they've just got the knack of enjoying Paradise. And I thought of all the birds in Liverpool, you know, and we've flowershops enough there, and not all those ruddy biting flies. The Mahawhatsit—"

"Manishtana."

"Eh. He told us, he did, that the flies are part of the oneness of one and the threeness of three, and that the man of spirit makes himself think the ruddy flies aren't there. It's a good idea, I'd say, but I'd have to be smoking day and night before I could ignore it when I've a fly up my bleeding nose."

"I love your records," Phaedra said.

He looked longingly at her. "Ah, girl," he said. To me he said, "She's yours, is she?"

"She's mine."

"Ah, you're a fine bloke. We'll stop in New York, but only long enough to kiss the ground hello. Our birds are in Liverpool, y'know. Flowers are fine, but birds are better. Birds are worlds better than flowers."

"Amen," I said.

Chapter Sixteen

❀ ❀ ❀

"Murder in London," the Chief said. *"Rumors of illegal* entry in half the capitals of Europe. Riots in Kabul."

He lowered his eyes. I had managed, miraculously enough, to be back at my apartment for a full two days before one of his messenger boys brought me word from him. Now we were in his room at a midtown Manhattan hotel where he was registered under a *nom de guerrefroide*. He was drinking a glass of scotch. I had a glass too, but I was letting it evaporate.

"I don't want much," he said. "Just a partial explanation. I suspect we can cover for you in Britain. As long as you're here and they're there, it shouldn't be an overwhelming problem. The top men can decide not to attempt extradition, and the underlings will let that sort of irregularity pass without making too much noise. But I *would* like to know what happened."

I couldn't blame him. He did think I was working for him, and if that was the case, it only made sense that I should let him know what sort of work I had done. His men, of whom I may or may not be one, depending upon one's point of view, enjoy more than the usual amount of autonomy. No written reports in triplicate, no countersigns and passwords, nothing but the maximum use of individual initiative carried out, hopefully, for the good of God and Country, though not necessarily in that particular or-

der. So he never asked for much, but he did have the right
to find out what the hell I had done, and why.

So I told him.

Well, I ought to qualify that. The general story, the way
you read it (unless you just happened to open the book to
this present page out of the blue, in which case close it,
please) does not make it look as though everything that
happened took place out of deepset motives of sheer patri-
otism. So I didn't think it would do my personal image
any particular good to let him know just how offhand the
whole bloody business had been.

I did tell him that I left the country for personal
reasons. But somewhere along the line imagination took
over from historical sense, and the story he got began to
part company with the truth.

Arthur Hook, I explained, was a conscious agent of
the communist conspiracy. By shipping potential white
slaves to Afghanistan, he was helping Russian agents inside
that country raise money for subversive purposes while at
the same time striking at the roots of the purity of the
women of the free world.

I looked at him, and that seemed to go over well
enough, so I gritted my teeth and went on with it. After I
learned all of this, I told him, I had to kill Hook so he
couldn't inform his confederates. Then I managed to
infiltrate myself into the mass of Soviet agents inside England and leave the country with them, although at the
last minute they found me out. From them I learned the
details of the plot in Afghanistan. Patriot that I was, I
realized it wasn't enough merely to rescue an innocent
American girl from the clutches of communist white-
slavers. I also had to quell the commie coup.

(It's embarrassing to write this down. Forgive me.)

With the aid of pro-Western elements in Kabul, I went
on, the revolt was nipped in the bud, crushed to a pulp
the day before it was scheduled to break out. The Russian
Embassy, traditional setting for scheming and subversion,
was now a heap of stones bearing no demonstrable relationship each to the other. The leaders of the would-be

putsch would lead no more putsches. A typical band of commie cutthroats, including not only sly Russians but the worst sort of European scum, they had literally been torn to pieces by an irate mob of freedom-loving Afghans.

"And so," I concluded, "I think it turned out fairly well, Chief. I never expected to get involved in anything that elaborate—"

"You never do."

"—or of course I would have let you know in advance what I was getting into."

"Mmmm," he said. He finished his drink and started to refill our glasses, then looked at me in surprise when he noticed that I had not yet finished mine. He glanced accusingly at me, and I drank my drink, and he poured more whiskey for each of us.

"Your track record," he said, "has always been good."

I didn't say anything.

"And I don't suppose this is actually *bad*, is it?"

"Well—"

He took a deep breath and let it out slowly. "But there is something I ought to tell you, Tanner. Something you ought to know. Something—well, unusual."

"Oh?"

"Slight miscalculation on your part, actually."

"Oh?"

"Rather serious, actually."

"Oh?"

He swung his chair around and looked at the window. I drank a little of my scotch. I was beginning to feel the need for it.

Without turning he said, "Tanner? The coup in Afghanistan. Not theirs, you see."

"Sir?"

"Ours."

"Ours?"

"Ours. Oh, not *ours* ours. Or of course you'd have known about it. No, not our department's sort of show, not by a long shot. Don't approve myself, as you well know. No, this was the personal property of the Boy Scouts."

I almost swallowed my tongue. I swallowed scotch instead. I said, "The CIA."

"Quite."

I didn't say anything.

"Afghan government's been neutralist, you see. Been accepting devil of a lot of aid from the Russians. New road, I understand—"

"If you saw the other roads, you'd understand why they accepted it."

"Don't doubt it. At any rate, someone at the Agency decided the government was playing it a bit too cozy with the Soviets. As they interpreted it, there would be a Red takeover within the year. They decided to anticipate events by staging a pro-Western takeover before the Russians were in position for a move."

"And the men in Kabul—"

"Were CIA operatives."

"But they were Russians. And Eastern Europeans. And—"

He was nodding. "Inherited that whole crew after the last war," he said. "Ukrainians, White Russians, that whole lot. Every secret agent type in Eastern Europe who was anti-Soviet came into the OSS after the war and then went CIA when the new outfit was formed. Collaborationists, a lot of them. No doubt about it. Pocket Hitlers, that type. But many of them were very valuable to the Agency."

"Uh," I said. I remembered assuring the Vulgar Bulgar that I was a devoted Russian myself. And afterward he and his bully boys redoubled their efforts to kill me. This had made little sense to me then. It made more sense now, although it didn't make me any happier.

"Well, this isn't good," I said.

"Oh?"

"I mean, well, I got a lot of men on our side killed. The CIA's men, that is. And I thought I was crushing a Commie plot, whereas I was actually crushing one of our own plots. An anti-commie plot, that is. Move. Coup. Whatever the hell it is."

"I think you might safely call it a plot."

"Er," I said. I choked back a burst of hysterical laughter. Hysteria seemed called for; laughter did not. I drank the rest of my drink. The Chief turned to look at the window again, then turned around to face me. I looked at his pudgy hands, his round face.

As I looked at him, he slowly began to smile.

The smile widened. The lips parted, and a chuckle came out. The chuckle turned into a laugh.

My jaw fell.

"Tanner," he said, "I'll tell you something. I think it's very goddamned funny."

"It is?"

"Of course it is." He began laughing some more. "The Boy Scouts wanted to stop a Russian takeover, didn't they? Well, the Russians won't get a foot in the door in that country in the next century. They don't even have an embassy any more, the poor bastards. There's a rumor the Kabul government's going to ask Moscow to take their road back, for heaven's sake. How on earth would you go about taking a road back?"

"I don't know, sir."

"Neither do I." He laughed again. "And the Russians—oh, this is precious—the Russians don't know how it happened either. They think the dead men *were* agents of theirs after all. Undoubtedly half of the men on their embassy staff were operatives, and as they died with the rest—well, you may well imagine the confusion in the Kremlin."

"I may well imagine," I said.

"Each of the Soviet agencies is accusing the other of prime responsibility for the situation. There will probably be a purge, perhaps several purges. And at least one of the agencies is trumpeting it about that Peking is responsible for what happened. That the Chinese were attempting to discredit Moscow on her own doorstep." He snorted. "So far everyone's gotten a bit of the blame except the International Zionist Conspiracy. And the United States."

"Then it turned out well," I said, slowly.

"It turned out perfectly. Except for the Boy Scouts, who lost a few reliable men."

"They weren't a particularly nice lot," I said.

"No, I don't suppose they were."

"Not at all."

"Well," he said. He sighed heavily. "I do think we ought to keep your role in this debacle completely quiet. As far as I can tell, the CIA ops in Kabul never got in touch with headquarters at Langley. They kept them wholly in the dark insofar as your presence was concerned. This is all to the good. As far as the Agency is concerned, their men made a bad error, got themselves knocked over by patriotic Afghans intent upon maintaining their neutrality, and the U.S. lucked out in that Kabul thinks they were Russians. Complicated, isn't it? All it adds up to is that we should keep quiet about this. I trust you'll do so?"

"Oh, definitely."

"And the girl? You did bring her out, didn't you?"

"She's a sort of private operative of mine," I said. "Actually she helped me penetrate the cover of that white-slaving operation to begin with. We won't have to worry about her."

"Good, good." He got to his feet, approached, extended his hand. We shook briefly. "You won't get a medal for this one," he said. "One of those exploits that must remain forever untold, as it were. But as far as I'm concerned, Tanner, you've done a good job." He began laughing. "Those Boy Scouts," he exploded. "I can just imagine the look on their silly faces—"

So when I got back to the apartment the phone was ringing. I made my usual mistake. I answered it.

"Mr. Tanner?"

"Long Numbel," I said. "This Brue Stahl Hand Raundley."

"Mr. Tanner, I know this is you. Don't tell me about laundries. I don't care from laundries."

I said, "Hello, Mrs. Horowitz."

"So I call you to find my Deborah for me and what do you do? A sinful woman you make of her."

"Uh."

"So when will you make an honest woman of her, eh, Tanner? Eh? I am alone in the world, Horowitz is dead, I'm alone, I've got nobody but Deborah. So I shouldn't lose a daughter, Tanner. I should gain a son, Tanner. You understand?"

"Deborah's not here, Mrs. Horowitz."

"Tanner, to you I'm talking."

"She went to the zoo, Mrs. Horowitz. I'll tell her you called."

"Tanner—"

I hung up, and before she could call back I took the phone off the hook. The door opened. I turned around, and it was Phaedra.

"Hi," she said. "You're back from your appointment."

"No, this is my astral projection. The Manishtana taught me how to do it."

"You do it very well, then. What's the matter with the phone?"

"Your mother was on it," I said.

"Oh."

"Where's the kid?"

"Downstairs," she said. "Playing with the Puerto Rican kid. Mikey."

"He's not in school?"

"It's Chanukah."

"I should have realized," I said. I looked at the phone. It was making that whirring noise that it makes so that you'll know that you didn't hang it up. The telephone company evidently can't believe that a person might want his phone off the hook for a reason. The telephone company never had a girl friend that had a mother.

I looked at Phaedra. She was taking off all her clothes.

I looked at the phone again. It had stopped whirring,

and now an operator was shouting at me to hang up the
receiver. Then there was some loud clanking, and then the
operator started in again.

"Listen to that woman," I said.

"I think she's a recording."

"They all are."

So I hung up the phone to stop the noise, and I reached
for Phaedra, and she giggled and purred, and the phone
rang.

The more things change . . .

At 2:30 one fine December afternoon I ripped the telephone out of the wall.